SHERLOCK HOLMES AND
THE MENACING METROPOLIS

*fighting fear and foreboding in the world's foremost
metropolis with the world's greatest detective*

Allan Mitchell

Paperback ISBN 978-1-78092-888-3
ePub ISBN 978-1-78092-889-0
PDF ISBN 978-1-78092-890-6

Published in the UK by MX Publishing
335 Princess Park Manor, Royal Drive,
London, N11 3GX www.mxpublishing.co.uk

Cover design by www.staunch.com

INTRODUCTION

Those who have ever turned down an invitation to accompany Holmes and Watson on their adventures are those who have never stepped back in time to experience the world of the later Nineteenth Century - a time when most people still touched the earth every day - a time when artificial actually meant hand-crafted - a time of horses and blacksmiths - a time of coal and coke - a time of smoke and sweat -a time of raw power, great change, great promise, great doubt - a time before people would fly above the Earth and beyond it – a time when knowledge of the Earth was just small enough for the Human mind to hold.

Powered by the steam engine, the century saw distance become ever less daunting as ships powered their ways against currents, tides and winds, and when trains pushed time and horses aside in the rush – even the practice of timekeeping became centralised away from local custom and control to fit in with the all-important metropolis-based train timetable to which all human life was increasingly having to bow.

If the rate of transport of people and goods had increased, the transfer time for ideas and information became unbelievably shortened as the telegraph operators tapped incessantly away, eroding the time more and more and spreading wire tentacles further and further each year. With the help of its younger telephonic cousin, the telegraph provided almost instantaneous communications and placed the average human in a subservient role – the telegram demanded an instant response and the telephone was answered without delay.

The Nineteenth Century was accelerating its way toward the Twentieth but Arthur Conan Doyle was able to stop time for his contemporary readers, if only for a few precious hours in a busy and demanding week during which change was otherwise both continuous and confusing. For us, as modern readers, time is not only stopped, it is put into reverse until we can find that reassuringly pleasant past plateau on which we are able to pause and ponder, a plateau only a few decades in breadth and open only to ourselves, Holmes and Watson and an assorted supporting cast of interesting characters who seem able to move back and forth and side to side in time and space according to the will of Arthur Conan Doyle and, of course, ourselves.

Not quite the unbelievable super-hero of modern times, Sherlock Holmes none-the-less displayed powers of mental dexterity well beyond the scope of normal people – he observed while others only saw, he knew what others never suspected and he deduced what others were incapable of construing. He did all this by collecting and cataloguing the essence of past cases, looking beyond the commonplace, questioning the seemingly obvious and observing patterns of behaviour which pointed to irregularity. Sherlock did not need a checklist to determine what was significant, he instinctively saw through the problem and knew the answer – he was just Sherlock ... is Sherlock!

CONTENTS

SHERLOCK HOLMES AND THE MENACING METROPOLIS

THE HOMECOMING

After solving relatively straightforward mystery concerning series of South Downs apiarian attacks, Holmes' passion for The Chase had been rekindled and he recognised that his retreat to the world of bees had been premature. His Public, as well, had become desperate for news of his successes against the forces of criminality and Watson had travelled with news of a new and generous offer by The Strand whose sales had plummeted in the absence of his reports. Convinced that he could now return home in triumph and finally cured of his obsession with his arch-enemy, Professor Moriarty, that fiend he had seen fall to his death in the surging cauldron at the base of the Reichenbach Falls, Holmes, accompanied by the loyal and stalwart Watson, boarded the train for the Great Metropolis.

It had been a bad few months for Holmes, his confidence had been shaken and his resolve had faltered, his name had been ridiculed and his reputation had been reduced to tatters. He had suspected the outrages on the Moors to have been some diabolical diversion away from something more sinister, something unfathomable until it dawned on him that he might have been the object of the unspeakable acts, acts designed to draw him in and face the limits of his abilities. The agent of the atrocities, a huge grizzly bear, had been destroyed, undoubtedly, but the diabolical mind behind the outrages was still at large. Holmes' deductive mind could allow a single solitary possibility: that Moriarty had survived the fall and had returned to seek satisfaction and victory in the Great

Sleuth's ruin. Events overtook Holmes and Watson convinced him that he should retire to the South Downs and raise bees, his often-stated plan for his declining years, but destiny could neither be ignored nor denied. None-the-less, his mind and body had been rested from the greater evils he had faced on the moors of Devon and the streets of London and, though he had not recognised the signs in himself, Sherlock Holmes had been reborn in spirit.

On returning to Baker Street after an impromptu victory walk through London's streets, however, Holmes was appalled and Watson was dumbstruck on finding a taunting message pinned to the door of 221B....

"My Dear Doctor Watson, when bear hunts you desire,
Is it Holmes you'd profess or Maurie Hardy, Esquire?"

A shocked and dismayed Watson, finding his voice after a few interminable seconds, looked directly into the face of the Great Sleuth and spoke ....

"Good God! My Dear Holmes. This just cannot be true.
If this man is alive we must search for a clue
Which might lead us to where such a demon resides
Before he can commit any more homicides."

"Quite so." replied Sherlock, *"But we must take care*
To proceed without seeming to take the man's dare
For we cannot afford to fall into his trap -
We are Pawns on a board – we're in Check to this chap."

"So we must up our game – change to Knights on a quest
And ride forth to do battle and pledge not to rest
Till this foe has been vanquished, his armour removed
And a case brought against him to have his guilt proved."

"When that happens, I'll be there to topple that King
And to shout out 'Checkmate!' which will then start to bring,
To the city, some semblance of order and law -
For, finding that note was, for me, the last straw."

"Quite so!" replied Watson, "But do not be fooled
For, in all forms of evil, the man has been schooled.
He's devious, Sherlock, as sly as a stoat
And, if he feels you're winning, he'll go for your throat."

"You must not play his game for his rules are not fixed -
His tactics will vary, his ploys will be mixed.
Chess is War, you must know, so you should not be vain -
Be prepared to adapt or you'll surely be slain."

Sherlock ripped off the note - said to Watson, *"It's time*
We regrouped to go fighting this master of crime.
We must show our resolve and, to panic, not stoop
And we must be prepared, for we know he will swoop."

"Get your key, Doctor Watson, and open that door.
Let us say to the world that I'm back from the Moor.
I have had a good holiday after that case
And, now, all refreshed, I am ripe for The Chase."

The pair stepped through the door and ascended the stairs
Just like two wily foxes returning to lairs
After ranging all night for a succulent yield
Of some rabbit or duck in a far-away field.

They would go through the motion of licking their lips
And pretend to be resting while coming to grips
With the problem they faced – they would talk until dawn
Of reducing this King to a snivelling Pawn.

But first they would gather the facts as they stood -
They'd look back on events and get rid of deadwood
And keep only those details and facts which they knew
To be true, absolutely – though these were quite few.

A mortified Watson, to Holmes, said, *"My Friend,*
What is there I might say which could ever defend
What I said on the Moors? I can only confess
I had thought that your mind was a bit of a mess."

"The fault is mine, Watson," Sherlock then insisted,
"If I'd been less forceful, you'd not have resisted
As much as you did to my outlandish notion -
I, myself, should have known it would cause a commotion."

"But I am a logician, my mind operates
In a logical manner and, so, separates
What is known absolutely from notions diverse
Lacking logic - unsound and overtly perverse."

"I have often said, Watson, whatever remains,
After one has examined and gone to great pains
To remove the impossible, one must take as fact
And, however improbable, upon this must act."

"What remained, in this instance, I knew couldn't be
For I fought with the man and I saw him as he
Toppled over the precipice into the spray
Of the great cataract which then took him away."

"I knew no one could ever live through such a fall -
Nobody could ever survive it at all.
In my mind's eye I see the man bounce off a rock.
How could any frail human survive such a shock?"

"My mind was in turmoil - two facts which opposed
One another in logic could not be supposed
To be able, at one point in time, to exist
Although, rejecting either, my mind would resist."

"The deviousness, that brutality, cold,
Made my mind exclude all but an enemy, old.
This thought, I resisted – no sense could be made -
But the thought became something I could not evade."

"But where was the motive, the causative link
In the chain of events? This had caused me to think
That some external factor, that link, had to be
And the only new external factor was me."

"There are two possibilities which must contend
For the truth of the matter - one must, in the end,
Prevail over the other to show us the way
To the source of the evil which brings such dismay."

"Moriarty is dead! So, then, who wrote that note?
Who knew we were returning from places remote?"
Sherlock mused, *"And who'd want to go to the trouble*
Of posing as him or his posthumous double?"

"Moriarty's alive! Well, if that is the case,
How did he survive the impact at the base
Of the Reichenbach Falls? For if he had done that,
He'd have needed the multiple lives of a cat."

"Both cannot be true but it does seem to be
That somebody is trying to bamboozle me
And to make me look foolish and addle my brain
Till, from further detection, I'd have to refrain."

Watson spoke resolutely, "*Both well may be true
But, for that to be so, you would have to construe
That the name Moriarty belongs to another.
That evil professor – he did have a brother.*"

"*Watson, that's it! Well, perhaps, it could be
That this brother is taking out vengeance on me.*"
Exclaimed Sherlock, excited, his great mind afire
With thoughts of reprisal and outcomes most dire.

Holmes was just on the verge of expanding this when
A sharp rap on the door and a soft "*Gentlemen!*"
Had proclaimed the arrival of one who had longed
For her tenant's return to where he had belonged.

Mrs Hudson came in with refreshments and cheer
For her tenant, returning, like some buccaneer
From a voyage to places unknown and exotic -
She walked in on a scene which was rather chaotic.

"*Mister Holmes, I insist you get rid of that frown -
Your face has the look of an upside-down clown.
You've been absent for ages – it's time to rejoice,
So I don't wish to hear a disparaging voice.*"

"*I've been stocking up treats and awaiting the day
Doctor Watson would bring you to London to stay
Where you truly belong – I have opened some wine
And have little indulgences, rather divine.*"

"*On my tray, I've three glasses so, if you'll permit,
These two, I will fill; to the third add a bit
For myself, and then offer a home-coming toast:
Sherlock Holmes, you're a tenant of whom I may boast.*"

"Here's to you, Mister Holmes - welcome back to the city.
You've been sadly missed and it would be a pity
To lose such a person as you to some bees -
If you hadn't come back, we'd have begged on our knees."

"Thank you, Mrs Hudson, I am glad to be back.
The Police Force, I notice, has gotten quite slack."
Replied Holmes while deciding on which tasty treat
He'd select from all those they were given to eat.

"Then I'll leave you both to it, whatever that is -"
Mrs Hudson declared, just as Watson ate his
Third or fourth slice of cake and he sipped on his wine,
"Your appetites, clearly, are bigger than mine."

Holmes and Watson dug in to this fare, culinary,
Which both had considered quite unnecessary
Although welcome, indeed – Mrs Hudson could cook
And the sleuths would eat better than most any crook .

For a worry-free hour, Watson barely spoke;
Sherlock sipped on his wine and declared he would smoke
His magnificent pipe and enjoy all the sounds
Of the traffic which plied Baker Street and surrounds.

In his mind, Holmes would file current fears in a tray
Which he'd place on a table so, later that day,
He'd be able to find, in good order, his notes,
While he'd tease Doctor Watson with fanciful quotes.

Holmes delighted in banter which often would serve
To massage every neuron and sharpen each nerve
In his brain till it glowed and had duly acquired
The extremely fine edge which the Great Sleuth required.

"*My conjecture,*" said Sherlock, "*is that very soon*
We shall see on this planet and, maybe, the moon
Gallant types who've courageously learned how to fly
When, their fleets, all mechanical, take to the sky."

"*Utter balderdash, Holmes!*" declared Watson as cake
From his mouth went exploding and dollop and flake
Went all over the dressing gown Holmes often wore -
Holmes yelled as he ducked, "*Please Watson, no more.*"

Without cake, Watson shouted, "*That thought, I'd defy -*
We'd have feathery wings if we'd been born to fly.
Now you say that somebody will fly 'round the planet
Like some misbegotten mechanical gannet."

"*A balloon full of hot air we've all seen to float*
Amid clouds in the heavens like some wayward boat
Taking people aloft and away," Sherlock stated.
Watson countered with, "*Hot air - you should be deflated.*"

"*Apart from which, Holmes, there's no air on the Moon*
And it would be the waste of a good afternoon
For someone to go floating off into the sky
And find he couldn't breathe and then die wondering why."

"*And why, to the Moon, would someone wish to travel?*
Only someone whose mind had begun to unravel
Would go there and ever expect to return.
Would we fly to the Sun and expect not to burn?"

"*There's a new age afoot, Watson, just look around*
And you'll see many signs of a movement profound."
Declared Holmes, while considering great sacrifices
Involved in inventing these modern devices.

"From petroleum drawn from deep under the ground
We will soon get the power to drive, all around,
Horseless carriages which will be set into action
By burning the volatile gasoline fraction."

"Holmes, "recoiled Watson, "I've heard how they splutter.
I know what the cabbies of London would utter
Should one dare appear in our thick London traffic -
It would be most unpleasant - decidedly graphic."

"But remember, "quipped Holmes, "it was not long ago
When the typical Englishman would have said 'No'
To the thought that a horse might, someday, be replaced
By a moving steam kettle which had it outpaced."

"Our own gracious Queen and her consort took pride
In our formative railways and went for a ride
As a very young couple and showed us, that day,
That the railways of Britain were here and would stay."

"So, why should we not, on a well prepared road,
Have a carriage which doesn't have horses to goad
To get heavy iron shoes to go clipping and clopping?
Not to mention the stuff all those horses keep dropping."

"Holmes, you're a dreamer, "said Watson, alarmed,
"I admit, with new gadgets, we all have been charmed.
But we'll never be free of our need of the horse -
Were that ever to happen, there's be great remorse."

"And even the bicycle, Holmes, you'd admit
Cannot replace the horse when one needs to permit
It to find its way home on a dark, stormy night
And its rider, with drink, is a little too tight."

"And I challenge those riders atop of two wheels
Or of four, for that matter, to keep even keels
When they're crossing a field or fording a stream -
To get any machine to do that is a dream."

"If your carriage gets hungry, the thing cannot munch
Any grass at the side of the road for its lunch.
They're just devilish by every criterion;
Horseless carriages – humbug – they'll never catch on!"

"I declare," stated Watson, *"that Mother England*
Is a nation, majestic and regal and grand;
It's the pinnacle of what a nation should be
And there's no other place that is better for me ."

"And the horse was the beast upon which grandeur rode -
The beast behind which all those unmounted strode
After enemies fleeing through bramble and gorse -
England's glory was won on the back of a horse!"

Sherlock smiled and then stated, *"My Friend, I agree*
That this nation of ours is a power set free.
England's at the forefront but, in England, we feel
We are powered by steam and are masters of steel."

Mrs Hudson stepped in on this forthright discussion
And stunned both its parties with northern percussion:
"Now, the both of you sometimes talk absolute rot
For the fellow who first conquered steam was a Scot."

"It was Scots built the lighthouses, drained all the mines,
Made great engines to drag heavy loads up inclines;
They macadamised roads so, to drive on, they're fit -
You Johnnies-Come-Lately down south must admit."

"They made passenger steamboats with hulls iron-clad
While, in England, some old sailing boats were the fad;
All the useful inventions this country has got
Were developed, as likely as not, by a Scot."

"Quite so!" replied Sherlock, *"And very well stated.*
The Scots' contributions can't be over-rated.
We are all in the shade of a dazzling light
When an intellect, northern, shines ever so bright."

"Well, enough of this, Watson; there's thinking to do -
We have serious work which we must attend to.
There's a fiend on the loose and his goose we must cook
Or at least help Police bring the fellow to book."

THE FACT

With their frivolous banter put deftly aside,
Holmes and Watson, together, then had to decide
On a firm plan of action based only on fact
With no spurious rumours allowed to distract.

They would state what they knew and consider the rest
But would not list a fact till it passed a strict test;
They'd list, in three columns marked "Yes, Maybe, No",
Every detail recalled from that case, months ago.

They would delve even further back into the past;
To the time when Sherlock has assumed that, at last,
He was rid of his old arch-adversary and
He could start to dismantle his criminal band.

Watson felt it a treat that he had been permitted
A view at Holmes' mental processes, admitted
To be quite astute and extremely insightful -
Holmes needed his help to fight evil so frightful.

"Devil's Advocate, Watson, I need you to be -
A voice which would challenge all notions from me
And ensure that my thinking is clear and concise."
Expressed Holmes with his need for inquiry, precise.

Watson said to his friend, *"Holmes, you've only to ask*
For I'm ready to take on that challenging task.
Advocatus Diaboli, from here on, I am -
We'll retain what is real and reject what is sham."

"I have often said, Watson, that you are the light
Which can guide me to places which otherwise might
Be enveloped in darkness, obscured from view -
You're a beacon." Holmes stated with fervour, anew.

"As for me, I'm vessel, awash and afloat
Out at sea in the darkness - one small flimsy boat
Seeking haven from danger, direction to port,
And a beacon to follow is what I exhort."

"My thoughts are inspired, my mind looks beyond
To what most do not see and, so, it will respond
To the tiniest detail, that piece out of place,
The absence of logic, the flimsiest trace."

"But Watson, your mind has been differently trained -
It will not accept notions until they're explained;
So, in trying to satisfy what you require,
My mind gets the insight that it would desire."

"This makes us, together, a power, you know -
Sherlock Holmes seeking facts shining out in the glow
From John Watson, the Beacon, the Giver of Light -
It's no wonder that criminals quiver in fright."

"So, let's start with the Reichenbach Falls when I fought
With a man who, in all probability, thought
That he'd cause me to topple and cause my demise.
Was this man dressed in some Moriarty disguise?"

"Or was it, in fact, the Professor who fell
And was dashed on a rock jutting out of the swell?
It may have been him or some stand-in, instead,
But I'm sure, absolutely, that someone was dead."

"Well, that must be a 'Maybe' at this point in time."
Declared Watson on whether the Master of Crime
Could be known to be dead or to still be alive.
"Perhaps later, we will, at a verdict, arrive."

"Now, what of that brother from whom you defended
My actions when all thought my life had been ended
As well as the life of that Master of Crime."
Said Sherlock, his mind ticking over, sublime.

"That's right," replied Watson, *"he wrote to the Press*
And asserted his brother had suffered duress
From what he claimed was persecution of one
Who was just a Professor to whom wrong was done."

"That's when I went to bat for my old absent friend
Who was certainly missing but who, in the end,
Had been hot on the trail of those in that gang
Who'd done things for which many of them had to hang."

16

"While you were away feigning death, I'd relate
The last words, so I thought, which I would dedicate
To the memory of one, Sherlock Holmes, and refute
All the slanderous lies on that man's great repute."

"At the time, I was furious, also distressed,
And was rather determined to have it impressed
On the minds of the Public that you had, quite gladly,
Your life, sacrificed, for all that you loved, sadly."

"It's occurred to me, only as we've been speaking,
And as, at my memories, you have been tweaking,
That this brother might simply have been playing games
For, unless I'm mistaken, he signed his name 'James'!"

Holmes broke in at that moment with, *"Did he, indeed?*
Is that truly the case? We must confirm, with speed
How that letter was signed, though, unless I am wrong,
The newspapers would not have retained it for long."

Holmes continued excitedly, saying, *"Perhaps*
Moriarty'd been wearing two different caps
Or had made a mistake in his communications.
What should we infer? This has great implications."

"We must check this out fully," said Sherlock, excited,
"A mistake such as this would have simply invited
The fellow to mute any further response,
Find a haven in which he might, himself, ensconce."

"Can you check in your manual for mention of one,
Colonel James Moriarty - I'd venture there's none
To be found in those long lists of honour and fame -
But there could be a Colonel of different first name."

17

"There is a James listed." said Watson, *"However,*
One so badly wounded in battle he never
Went back to the Colours - he went on the list
Of those repatriated; well, you get the gist."

"Indeed I do , Watson, but is there another?
Somebody who served and who might be the brother
Of him I had thought we were rid of forever?"
Queried Holmes, *"Is there nobody listed, whatever?"*

"No one I can see who might quite fit the bill -
There's a George listed here who, it seems, got his fill
At the Waterloo battle when, it says, that the French
Blasted him and his comrades right out of their trench."

Sherlock said, after seeing that Watson was done,
"Well, I feel we might discount that Waterloo one -
He sounds rather gallant but also quite dead -
We must look at that one, badly wounded, instead."

"We should also consider that man from the Moor;
'Maurie Hardy' he wrote on that note on the door
With the two words 'profess or' completing the taunts -
It would seem that the fellow's returned to his haunts."

"But who was that fellow? Was he Moriarty?
Or was he some devious underworld smarty
Who assisted the man in some odd enterprise?
Perhaps he was Colonel Moran in disguise."

"Well, so much for facts." exclaimed Watson, dismayed
At the way which their thoughts had been veering away
From the itemisation of things which they found
To be facts, absolute. Was their method unsound?

18

"Real life can be messy." said Holmes, *"It's a treat*
If the simplest of cases is tidy and neat.
We must look for anomalies in the great jumble
Of lies and deception where felons might fumble."

"When someone signed 'James' to that hostile letter,
It might be the case that we could have no better
Indicative fumble to point to a fact -
We must find out who wrote this and then we must act."

"Remember the bear on the Moors when you shot
The great beast as it reared and then how you forgot
Every fanciful notion – the rumours were fake,
And the bear, in its rage, made a fatal mistake."

"Likewise, it could be, that as justice closed in
On that evil Professor, resources were thin
And he had to act quickly with no time to plan -
A fatal mistake for a well prepared man."

"He was hurt, that's a fact – we should give 'Yes' a tick
To the fact Moriarty's whole gang got a kick
Where it richly deserved it – he may have returned
Back to London to find his foul empire burned."

"So, the newspaper letters which tried to defame
My esteemed reputation and drag my good name
Through the gutter were possibly penned in great haste
As the man, of defeat, had his first bitter taste."

"There's a lesson, here, Watson, which you might record
And it is that the righteous can never afford
To underrate felons with freedom at stake,
But to overrate them is a greater mistake."

"Moriarty is fallible, that we can say,
Although that doesn't mean he won't act in a way
Which is scheming and devious, wily and sly -
He's had time to recover – that, we can't deny."

"That's assuming," said Watson, *"he's truly our man.*
We must not act in haste – if we do, then we can
Be as foolish as him and risk utter confusion.
We do not want to jump to a bitter conclusion."

"It's a working hypothesis, Watson, a guess,
And the one we'll proceed with, together, unless
It is shown we're in error when facts are collected
And these do not point to the end we expected."

"Well, what else do we know we can label as fact?
Is there something we know upon which we can act
And then have this explosive offender defused?"
Queried Watson, determined but somewhat confused.

"We know someone was down on those Moors, desolate;
It was someone determined to cause a great spate
Of despicable horrors on innocent sheep;"
Said Sherlock, *"Somebody with evil set deep."*

"Maurie Hardy he called himself, but we don't know
That it was Moriarty just trying to show
Me that he was so clever by making me fall
In the eyes of the Public – we don't know at all."

"But, we should list as fact that there is such a man
And we'll list him as Hardy, that is, till we can
Both resolve and confirm his identity, true -
If he is Moriarty, we must find the clue."

"He'll be watching us, Watson; or someone he pays
Will observe and report upon whether Holmes stays
In his Baker Street digs or goes out on the prowl -
We must watch for this watcher with eyes of an owl."

"But we can't stay indoors and expect to do battle
With evil like his - we must act and, so, rattle
The cage of this rat so that he will emerge."
Said Watson, *"And then, when he does, we'll converge."*

"He'll avoid his old haunts, so we must start from scratch."
Declared Sherlock, while striking a hesitant match
Several times on his boot sole – he needed to smoke -
A two-piper sitting, such problems invoke.

"Should we inform Lestrade in a way which will not
Cause a ruckus like last time when he said 'You've got
To be joking!' and had you turned out of the Yard?"
Asked Watson of Sherlock, *"Would that be too hard?"*

"That is what we must do." said Holmes, mortified,
"But such notions from me might be duly defied
By Lestrade who will, though proficient, convey
The fact that, superiors, he must obey."

"I fear we must tread very softly, My Friend,
For I'd wish to involve him but not to offend
His robust sense of duty and cause a new rift
Between us –one which would set our friendship adrift."

"You should leave it to me to make contact with him."
Said Watson, declaring, though not on a whim,
That, *"If you see him now, you will lead with your chin*
And the Yard might explode with a terrible din."

"Let's recap what we know and declare what we think
And plan what we should do to bring, up to the brink
Of defeat by the forces of justice, that man
Who can invent more evil than anyone can."

"I will take to Lestrade all such facts as we know
And, in manner quite logical, quietly show
To this able detective the dangers we face
And outline the grand plan we are setting in place."

"I will make several stops on the way to the Yard
For, if we're being watched, I must be on my guard.
I will call in on colleagues, the medical kind,
On some pretext or other - they surely won't mind."

"The final approaches, on foot, I'll complete
And I trust any stalker will never compete
With this Doctor for stealth in such secretive acts -
I will locate Lestrade and I'll give him the facts."

Watson walked down the steps to the hallway below
And tripped over a crate which was broad and quite low
And addressed to himself and his detective friend -
He said words which, if heard, would be sure to offend.

Watson undid the bindings and pried off the lid
And ripped out all the packing to see what it hid.
Twelve large jars of honey were packed in the crate -
He would retract his curses – it wasn't too late.

Holmes had heard the commotion and sprang to assist
In what manner he could but then had to resist
The temptation to laugh at his friend sitting squat
On the floor saying, *"Holmes you'll just never guess what."*

"We have twelve jars of honey to use and to share -
From the South Downs has come this delectable fare
Full of sweetness and sunshine – Mrs Hudson will flip -
Help me up, will you, Sherlock, I've shattered my hip."

"It's from Wilkinson-Hugh. Well, if that isn't grand.
He says here on this note that, in all of the land,
If there's one who, for justice, has made an impact,
His name would be Sherlock – take that as a fact."

THE TOWER

"It's an omen," said Watson, *"a definite sign*
That you're under the guidance of forces benign.
You are held in esteem by so many you've met
And Lestrade is among those, I'd certainly bet."

Watson managed to stand as his hip wasn't shattered
But it hurt everywhere that he thought that it mattered.
He said, *"Call me a cab, if you would be so kind.*
I may limp when I walk but I really don't mind."

Watson set off to visit Lestrade but would stop
And consult Doctor Denton, a bit of a fop
But a likeable fellow who said of his limp,
"Watson, you're walking around like a chimp."

"Are you here to consult me about what you've done
To your leg or your hip, or is it about one
Of your cases with Sherlock? I hear that he's back
And has veered off that silly apiarian tack."

Watson sat in a chair, his hip somewhat painful
Though, of his discomfort, he acted disdainful,
And said to his colleague, *"Well, Denton, My Friend,*
My hip hurts a little but, no doubt, will mend."

"I am here on a mission for Sherlock, in fact,
But I must exercise some significant tact
For I'm sure I'm being followed by forces malign
And I must, of my purpose, not give them a sign."

"Well, this is exciting," said Denton, aware
That his colleague, John Watson, would never declare
What his friend, Sherlock Holmes, was up to at the time -
He simply assumed he'd be battling crime.

"But your hip would appear to be quite bothersome.
I assumed, when I saw you, that's why you had come.
But you tell me you're dodging someone on your tail -
Let us see if we can't take the wind from his sail."

"You must borrow my cane – I just have it for show
And I'll send you right off to see someone I know
Who can help with the pain if, mobile, you must be -
There's no better apothecary than he."

"So, you ought to consult with my friend, Mr Porter -
When it comes to painkillers, he's just a ripsnorter.
He's sure to have something to have your pain ended
Though continued use would not be recommended."

"But is the stuff legal?" asked Watson, alarmed
That he might, from its usage, end up being harmed
Or, worse still, arrested; but Denton replied,
"It certainly is, unless Porter has lied."

"Go out the back door and, my coat, you should take,
And, that pitiful bowler you wear, could forsake
For that floppy peaked cap which I use when it rains -
Bring them back later on... without any blood stains."

With directions to Porter's apothecary,
John Watson, disguised as he thought necessary,
Stole out of his friend's humble medical rooms
Past a pile of his cleaner's old buckets and brooms.

The cane was of help and the clothes did the trick,
Or he thought they had done for he managed a quick
Look around in the lane and saw no one in wait -
He stepped out and moved off with a fumbling gait.

Through a little arcade which led to the next street,
He would move, hoping that he'd not happen to meet
Anyone that he knew who would stop him and talk -
He pulled down Denton's cap and proceeded to walk.

Within just a few minutes, the place Watson sought,
He would find and he hoped that, perhaps, Porter ought
To be able to dull the distress in his hip
By providing a potion from which he might sip.

After brief introductions, the note Watson took
From his pocket and gave it to Porter to look
At the message it held –it held more than he thought
And it said to give Watson all help that he sought.

"This note introduces John Watson, our friend,
And, without hesitation, I'd highly commend
Him to you as a client– he's damaged his hip
And he needs a concoction of yours he may sip."

Porter read the note quickly, showed Watson a chair,
And he said, *"As you've walked here, the chances are fair*
That the damage is not very serious, but
I will deaden the pain and I won't have to cut."

A wry smile from the stern face of Watson appeared
For he, too, knew his hip to be not, as first feared,
Badly injured, just jarred, with a bruise on its way,
So he then said to Porter, *"I'm grateful – good day."*

"Good day to you, also; I'm glad we have met,"
Replied Porter, while stretching his arm out to get,
From a high shelf, a jar labelled 'special, take care'
"This concoction won't take any time to prepare."

Two spoonfuls of that which, it seems, Porter treasured,
Into a small mortar, were carefully measured;
From a drawer came a pestle for grinding it fine -
Porter said, *"This concoction's a favourite of mine."*

"Should I ask what you're grinding, or should I not know?"
Queried Watson whose interest had started to grow;
Porter stared and replied, *"What this stuff is, as such,*
I would rather not say, but do not take too much!"

"It's kept only for friends with a need for its gifts
For I've found that a small amount frequently shifts
Any pain from the body, though large amounts can
Be a poison most deadly – be careful, Good Man."

"I'm a medical Doctor," John Watson replied,
"And familiar with poisons." he said as he spied
Porter grinding his 'stuff' to a powdery form
Saying *"This should be fine and, of course, uniform."*

In a half-filled decanter of water he'd mix
Half a spoonful of 'stuff' saying, *"This ought to fix*
Any pain you are feeling – the dose is correct
And there should be nothing untoward you'll detect."

"Here's some Wintergreen Oil which you might apply
To the skin 'round your hip; if you have a supply
You should use it ... well, you'd know all about that ...
When you're ready, we must have a really good chat."

"I've been jumping ahead of myself in my haste
But just take this 'stuff' with you – I do not like waste.
So I'll pour the remainder in this envelope
And nobody will know what's inside it, I hope."

"Now, Donald Porter's the name - Apothecary"
Declared Watson's new friend, *"And it's customary*
For two strangers to be introduced in this way
Before talk should commence, but it's backwards, today."

"John Watson M.D., Doctor Denton's my friend;
He said you'd be the one who'd have me on the mend
Or at least feeling better – he said you had ways
Of removing a difficulty without delays."

Porter took Watson's hand in a gesture of grace
And, with his other hand, made a double embrace
On the top of both hands clenched with friendship declared
And, into Watson's face, for a longish time, stared.

When the grips were relaxed, Watson, slightly bemused,
Thought about what had happened and silently mused
On just what had been meant; had he misunderstood?
"A two-handed handshake – bad omen, or good?"

"It's a club, Doctor Watson, one which you have been
Just invited to join – but a club never seen
By the Public, at large – it has members, quite few,
And we think that it's time that we had someone new."

"It's a club which exhibits considerable power
In quite subtle ways, and we call it The Tower -
The Tower of London to those in the know -
If you're interested, Doctor, there's much more to show."

"I don't know what to say." stuttered Watson, surprised,
"I had come seeking treatment as I'd been advised
By my friend, Doctor Denton, but seemed to have found
Some society, secret - perhaps underground."

Porter heard what he said and, then, close to his ear
He said softly to Watson, *"Some things you must hear*
Before I can reveal any work of 'our friends' -
If you don't wish to hear, then our discussion ends."

"I am not disinterested in your proposal,
I have ample time and it's at the disposal
Of agents of law and of order and good,"
Declared Watson, *"I do want that fact understood."*

Porter said, *"I agree and would never presume*
That you'd ever be otherwise, but would assume
That, because you were sent here by Denton, our friend,
You would be of the sort he could highly commend."

"The Tower of London has secrets it keeps -
Nothing sinister, mind you, but evil just seeps
Through the pores of our city – we offer a way
To plug up a few pores and keep evil at bay."

"Your reticence, Doctor, I do understand
We invite your involvement but do not demand.
There's one factor, however, to counter your fear -
Sherlock Holmes has been with us for many a year."

"Sherlock Holmes – one of you? Surely that isn't right.
I have worked with the man both by day and by night
And have never heard from him a word of your club."
Declared Watson, annoyed and suspecting a snub.

A sense of betrayal pervaded his mind -
"I'm sure Sherlock Holmes would not be so unkind
As to keep from a friend and a colleague like me
Such a secret as this –surely it cannot be."

"We are not vigilantes," said Porter, explaining,
"For ours is a mission to help in restraining
The outbreak and spread of all organised crime
In our city of London that's rife in our time."

"All our members are such that, from people they know
From all parts of the city, they filter the flow
Of diverse information, then meet to compare
And collate any knowledge of which to beware."

"Some members have contacts and clientele who,
In themselves, are no threat but who are likely to
Be affected in some way by impending crime -
They are good indicators, well, much of the time."

"We do not act on impulse - we must be restrained
And release of our knowledge won't be entertained
Unless it has been vetted and considered well;
Only then will The Tower decide who to tell."

"We must, too, decide what, for we are quite aware
That, when criminals plan, some will take extreme care
And might set up a trap to detect a weak link
In the chain they have forged and, on that, we must think."

"It is very fortuitous that you have come
For, although you and Holmes make a splendid twosome,
The Tower has eyes and a great many ears -
It's surprising how much that it sees and it hears."

"At its most recent meeting, The Tower proposed
That, if it was considered that you'd be disposed
To join with us, we would make a subtle approach
And to, then, of the matter of joining us, broach."

"There were reasons that we hadn't done this before,
Even though none of us could admire you more.
We rarely have members who work as a team -
It can hamper the flowing intelligence stream."

"They can't help but discuss anything either finds
And mull over whatever that is in their minds;
We have found to present basic facts is the best
Way to paint a broad picture which we can then test."

"We have outlets for any suspicions we form -
A quiet whisper to someone we trust is the norm.
But that one we can trust must be able to act
And not give us away, so he must show some tact."

"Any action that's taken should be indirect
For we don't want the evil we fight to detect
Any leakage of knowledge or hints gone astray -
Our effectiveness might disappear in a day."

"Sherlock Holmes is one outlet, but also will act
As a source which, as likely as not, is exact;
So, we'd like you to join us – we know you've the skill
And, to let down your comrades in arms, never will."

"But Holmes is a loner – unique in his ways -
And despite his connection with you, he displays
Bizarre ideas of teamwork and sharing and, thus,
We will mostly tell him more than he will tell us."

"Take what time you may need, Watson, answer us when
You've discussed it with Holmes and agreed; we can then,
As we greatly admire your marvellous ploys,
Include in our circle, both Baker Street Boys."

"The Baker Street Boys." Watson said with a chuckle,
"Such frivolous talk will be sure to unbuckle
Holmes' famous demeanour – he might take a fit
But I'm sure to have fun with the name for a bit."

"It's a little mind-numbing," John Watson admitted,
"I can see how somebody like Holmes would be fitted
Into such a body – his brain is acute,
His heart is sincere and his manner astute."

"I'll discuss it with Sherlock, I was going to
See Lestrade at the Yard but don't know what to do
For we have information it's vital he know
But perhaps, to The Tower of London, should show."

Porter said, *"First, to Holmes, it is better to talk.*
I will call you a Hansom, it's too far to walk
If someone's on your tail; then he'll only have seen
That, just for your hip's treatment, away you have been."

"For your hat and your coat, my lad I'll now send
With a message for Denton – he'll simply pretend
He's returning some package he's borrowed from me -
You can change in the back then away you can be."

Watson went back excited - to Sherlock he'd say,
"I have been to the Tower of London today.
It affords quite a view and I had quite a chat
But a Baker Street Boy will have known about that."

"The secret was one which was not mine to share
Unless all in the Tower agreed to declare
You a member, potential," Holmes had to reply,
"If you know of their work then you'll understand why."

"I was a bit miffed, but I'm over it now
And would like to join up if I'm told where and how."
Declared Watson determined to help as he might -
"I did not see Lestrade – should I see him tonight?"

"Not exactly tonight, Watson, but we'll attend
A most unusual dinner at which we'll amend
Its attendance list so that your name will be seen
Amongst Knights of the Tower." said Sherlock, quite keen.

"A Baker Street Boy and a Towering Knight
And in just a few hours – this gives me delight."
Watson thought to himself quite forgetting his hip,
"I'm just back from the Downs so I must get a grip."

"I will rest for a while and consider this change
In my circumstances – it's a little bit strange.
It would seem, with this offer, I'm now on a winner.
Holmes! You must tell me – it's formal, this dinner?"

THE DINNER

Well, the dinner was set for the following night -
Watson looked forward to it with utmost delight.
He had not the least notion of what to expect
But assumed he'd meet people, in some way, select.

It was formal, of course, as John Watson well knew,
And he spied from the Hansom, as slowly it drew
To a halt in a road he'd not heard of before
At what looked like a long-disused boot-maker's store.

*"What is this place, Holmes? I confess I've not been
In this part of the city and never have seen
Such a restaurant as this. Are you sure it's tonight?
This looks like a wonderful place for a fight."*

Sherlock said to his friend, *"This is just the first stop.
A four-wheeler will come and aboard it we'll hop
And proceed to pick up a few more of our friends
And you'll learn quite a lot before this evening ends."*

*"We never go straight to the place we will dine
So we leave about Seven and get there at Nine
And we change, at least once, the conveyance we use
So that, if we are seen, it is sure to confuse."*

When a covered four-wheeler appeared in the street
Holmes said, *"Here are two of the men you must meet.
We must pick up one more from a lane quite nearby
And two ladies will join us but, Watson, don't pry."*

*"Some people won't mind if you recall their names
But, you must understand, we are not playing games.
This is serious business, not social contact
And we must show, at all times, remarkable tact."*

"We will dine, we will chat, we will hint about things
We have seen and have heard and, in due time, this brings
A discussion of something a hint has suggested,
While we go about getting our dinners digested."

"The table at which we dine comfortably seats
Twenty-one; more than this, practicality beats
For we've found that this number of minds interact
In an optimal manner – too many distract."

"Our room is quite private, the restaurant is real
And delivers, I must say, an excellent meal;
The chef and proprietor know of our quest
And have sworn to say nothing - your mind, you may rest."

"We arrive as small groups, although some come alone,
For a large group like ours would stand out and be prone
To be stared at by curious, quizzical sorts
And would risk being mentioned in social reports."

"We've a lawyer, a judge, an old soldier and such,
Some know Official Secrets and can't say too much;
An apothecary and a doctor you've met;
There's a bookmaker, too, who will not take my bet."

"We've a dentist, a banker, an ex-mountaineer,
A Hansom cab driver and one engineer;
A stockbroker comes also, his hand on the pulse
Of big business quite hale or about to convulse."

"We've one ex-detective - a handy contact;
We've two station masters with knowledge exact;
We've a public house barmaid who always attends,
And a Cabinet Minister's wife – they're good friends."

"We've a couple of fellows with eyes on the docks;
We've a dressmaker fashioning stylish frocks;
There's me as you've learned – that's a total of twenty;
When we fill up a vacancy, then we'll have plenty."

"It's not what people tell us directly, you see;
Each collects from the field, like a foraging bee
Bringing pollen and nectar to flower and hive -
We share all we can carry when, back, we arrive."

"That's a quite motley lot, I must say," Watson quipped,
"It would seem that your group is superbly equipped
To glean snippets from everywhere right across this
Most magnificent menacing metropolis."

"Correct!" agreed Holmes, *"But we're seeking another.*
The recent demise of a most worthy brother
Who'd served us most diligently many a year
Left a gap – his replacement by you, voted clear."

As they spoke, the four-wheeler had stopped right beside
The illustrious pair causing Sherlock to stride
And to open its door and bid Watson, *"Get in*
And then make yourself comfortable." thwarting a grin.

Watson entered, though comfort was there, all around,
And said, feeling as though taken high off the ground
And was floating on clouds, *"Holmes, our seats are so soft.*
Is this one of those flying machines gone aloft?"

"So it is, my dear Watson, it's what London needs -
A four-wheeler pulled by two mechanical steeds
Which will haul it aloft – now move over, My Friend,"
Replied Holmes, *"for to get on this bird, I must bend."*

"Now, fly away, Driver, and find us that cloud
To where friends now await us – you've done us all proud
With this wonderful wagon, the top of the line,
And all for John Watson, a good friend of mine."

"It's for me?" stuttered Watson, *"But surely you jest.*
Why would anyone think I expected the best?"
Holmes replied, *"It is just how we show our esteem.*
You are more to our group than you think you may seem."

Watson went very quiet as, onward, they sped,
But he heard Sherlock saying, *"Come in tube fed,*
That is, after you've greeted the man of the hour -
He's a little reserved at the moment, not dour."

They had stopped to pick up two more passengers who
Were both climbing aboard when John Watson came to;
In deep thought, he'd not noticed the passing of time -
He was fixed in his mind on a notion sublime.

"Hello, Doctor Watson," in unison stated
Both Fenshaw and Williams, their eyes all fixated
Upon the embellishments of their conveyance
While keeping their innermost thoughts in abeyance.

Watson looked up and saw at least one face he knew.
It belonged to a lawyer quite glad to renew
An acquaintance of old he'd not seen for so long
And he took Watson's hand in a grip long and strong.

"It's Fenshaw, I know you - I'd never have guessed
You'd be part of this group, though, it must be confessed
This group's very existence was unknown before
Denton steered me into Porter's wonderful store."

"Ah! You've met our friend Porter – a character, true;
What is in his concoctions, I haven't a clue."
Declared Fenshaw, all smiles, *"But, at times, it's a must*
Though I think it's an extract of old fairy dust."

"But, where are my manners? Doctor Watson, please meet
Mr Wordsworth Yeats Williams of Threadneedle Street."
"Pleased to meet you." said Watson, *"A handsome address."*
The banker replied, *"Where I work, I confess."*

"But so much comes and goes, and a lot of loose talk
In surprising amounts, I will hear as I walk
Through those elegant halls on my way to the vaults -
So many, for chatter, have so many faults."

"Now, Driver, away," Sherlock said with a tap
On the side of the carriage, *"Now, there's a good chap."*
From outside, from the driver's seat, came the reply,
"I'll give you 'good chap' now sit back while I fly."

"An impudent fellow," said Watson, surprised
But did not utter more after Sherlock advised
Him that they were being driven by Richards and Co.,
Who could take them most anywhere they wished to go.

"John Richards, that's 'Rickety Jack' to his friends,
Provides all sorts of transport – his Company wends
Its way all over London with people and freight
And for Williams with what he calls 'pieces of eight'."

"He will drive us, himself, for he is one of us -
I suppose he could pick us all up in his bus
But we'd be too conspicuous riding as one,
And his old Hansom cab – well, it couldn't be done."

"Now, we've two to pick up, then our carriage is full
And our flesh and blood horses can finally pull
Us to Morrison's Warehouse – we've ladies to dine -
Mrs Tully and friend, Lady Margaret Devine."

"Mrs Tully hears all and she sees even more.
In her East London pub she gets punters galore
Who will cry on her shoulder, take over the bar,
Then get sodden and go, with their bragging, too far."

"There are lots of loose tongues in a bar-room, My Friend,
Near as many as are where a Lady must fend
For herself taking tea with the Cabinet-wives' set -
Those tongues might be loose but they're powerful, yet."

"Lots of influence, hidden, is exercised when
There are gathered the wives of those powerful men
Who would steer our great Empire spread overseas -
Do not under-rate all of those afternoon-teas."

"Much like Mrs Tully, Lady Margaret will spot
What is said over teacups and also what's not.
They are brokers of power, these powerful wives -
Their words may be soft but they use them like knives."

"That's so right," agreed Williams, *"but don't be amused*
Because many a stoush in the Lords was defused
By those very same tongues when they set out to heal
All those rifts caused by husbands with far too much zeal."

"But, Holmes, you made mention of horses, before -
Flesh and blood types, you said; and so, now, tell us more."
But Watson jumped in, saying, *"If you'd know why,*
Quite wrongly, Holmes says that one day we might fly."

"You're quite right, Doctor Watson, I'd think it unsound
To be further than we are, right now, off the ground."
Declared Fenshaw, *"If I went aloft, I'll admit*
That, at best, I would faint and, at worst, take a fit."

"Well, take a fit elsewhere, the ladies are here
And we won't go aloft to the high atmosphere
But all keep our feet firmly upon British soil,"
Said Holmes, with a grin, *"or our dinner may spoil."*

"Lady Margaret, Mrs Tully," said Richards, *"Good night.*
But I warn you, inside they are having a fight
About ladies with knives and of horses that fly
So, if you'd hop on board, I'm sure you'll find out why."

"It's that dashed Sherlock Holmes," Mrs Tully declared,
"He will set folks a trap and then have them all snared
And then dangled on hooks while they squabble and fight."
"It's worse," Richards said, *"he's got Watson tonight."*

With the ladies on board, they all went on their way
With a great deal of banter, enjoying the sway
Of their marvellous carriage, the clip and the clop
Of the horses in front till, at last, they would stop.

In a lane at the back of the place where they'd meet,
They alighted and walked in three pairs to the street
At the front where they'd enter in pairs to be led
To their table, upstairs, behind curtains, deep red.

Restaurateur, André, would greet them in French;
In daylight, however, the fellow would wrench
Back his nocturnal accent most felt was in-vogue -
Half Russian, half Cockney – the man was a rogue.

But a rogue amongst rogues in a city quite tough
In an industry in which some people got rough;
But André was wise, played the game as it came -
To show weakness in London would make one fair game.

Not part of their group, none-the-less, André would
Offer snippets of gossip which possibly could
Be of interest, great, to the gathering Tower -
André, in his way, was a towering power.

As the rest of the singles and pairs were arriving
André and 'The Chef' were both bent on contriving
A sumptuous meal – they would not be outdone
But it wouldn't be easy to please everyone.

'The Chef' was a Frenchman whose name was unknown
Or, so it was said by the ones who had grown
To enjoy the mystique of his magic cuisine -
Whatever it was, it would not be routine.

The Chef greeted the group, now all settled around
What some often referred to as their Table Round;
He proceeded to tell in his accented tone
That, a special menu, he had for them, alone.

If the fellow was French, well, no one really knew
But his food was delicious so nobody drew
Him aside to ask questions of origins Gallic -
The man had a temper and large knives, metallic.

Selections were made from The Chef's board of fare;
Then both Denton and Porter made Watson aware
Of the protocols followed – then dinners arrived
And no one could complain of his being deprived.

As twenty-one meals disappeared, one by one,
Sherlock rose from his seat, saying, *"Second to none!*
That's the way that I feel about someone we've sought
To be part of our group and who, with me, I've brought."

"John Watson M.D., both a colleague and friend,
Has a reputation I've no need to defend
For we all know his work and his character, too,
So I'll introduce him with no further ado."

"Please stand, Doctor Watson, your presence, alone,
Signifies that you've joined us." Holmes said with a tone
Which was close to being humble – unusual for him,
"Your are here on a mission and not on a whim."

Watson got to his feet, somewhat apprehensive
About how to respond – and being rather pensive,
He'd avoid public speaking like some deadly plague
So he started to speak trying not to sound vague.

"Well, thank you, My Friend, for that little tribute,
Though I feel that, today, I fell down through some chute
And emerged in a parallel world undetected
By most in this city, or even suspected."

"And it will be my pleasure - my duty, in fact,
To assist, as I might, anyone who would act
Against forces which menace this city so grand
And, of course, our great Empire, as one might demand."

Donald Porter stood up saying, *"Thank you 'Our Friend'*
For that's how we refer to each other to send
Any message quite subtle when we'd introduce
Any one whom we trust or intend to induce."

"We do not utter oaths or sign affidavits
For we all trust each other and know that each fits
With insight that's unique, quite as likely as not -
Now, right down to business, it's time that we got."

THE THREAT

With the table now cleared, save for coffee and port,
Mrs Tully then said, *"An unusual sort*
Of a man, well-attired, was recruiting a crew,
But of foreigners, only – to me, he was new."

"His broad accent was Northern, perhaps out of York,
And the way that he handled his knife and his fork
With his meal, and his manners, had caused me unease -
In my pub I'd be lucky for 'thank you' or 'please'."

"He spoke to a Dutchman, two Russians, I think,
And, on leaving, he gave me a shielded wink
As he paid with a Fiver and said, 'Keep the change'.
Well, that in itself, was decidedly strange."

"Then he pushed his forefinger right onto my lips
Saying 'things can get nasty if anything slips
Past those nice teeth of yours – understand what I say -
When I come here to talk, keep your ears well away'."

"He said he would be back and I said 'that is fine -
I don't want any trouble in this Pub of mine;
I want only the business that customers bring
And as long as they pay, I do not hear a thing'."

Bill Manson gave Waters an all-knowing look.
Being foremen, they knew, on the docks, such a crook
Had been trouble before but had long been away -
They did not want the fellow returning some day.

"Sounds like Percy the Ponce, a most pretentious git."
Uttered Manson, *"The man overdresses a bit*
But is only a puppet - though, trouble, be brings.
If he gave you a Fiver, someone's pulling strings."

"He's been seen near our docks in the past week or so
That's a place he's been warned that he never should go."
Added Waters, *"That weasel's a sly little creep,*
He needs dropping at sea at a spot good and deep."

"He is known to have thrown around money before
Dressed unlike any hard-working dock stevedore;
He sought muscle for something that wouldn't be petty -
He once got himself thrown off the end of a jetty."

"He's a man out of place – well, that's how it appears.
We should keep our eyes open and clean out our ears
As five pounds is a fortune to types such as he."
Declared Sherlock, *"The fellow is unknown to me."*

"He's done time in the Dart and he likes to act tough
Though I have to admit, if the man has enough
Of his cohorts behind him, there's trouble at hand."
Ex-Detective Jakes stated, *"A nasty brigand."*

"I once put him away for a burglary, though
While he talked like a hero, he folded like dough
When we spoke of the rope we might fit 'round his neck;
Then he cried like a baby – the man was a wreck."

"A quite dangerous wreck, I expect, he might be,"
Said Sherlock to Jakes, infuriated that he
Had been off keeping bees and had not been around
To be very much help at the great Table Round.

He had wanted to say, to the Tower, that he
Had experienced what might be a catastrophe
When he found a note pinned to his Baker Street door
With a message, most menacing, straight from Dartmoor.

But Holmes, his impulses being better controlled,
Would now mentally keep his report tightly rolled
And would wait for the moment the Knights might accept
Moriarty's survival a likely concept.

So he bit on his tongue and kept, close to his chest,
Any hint of what he had come there to divest;
He would find the right moment – rashness had a price -
Meanwhile, he would give Mrs Tully advice.

"Mrs Tully, there's danger afoot, so you must
Be aware that this man isn't one you can trust.
He would do you real mischief if he'd once suspect
Any deceit on your part, so be circumspect."

"You should keep your ears honed for the merest of clues
And report what you hear; then, as data accrues,
We might just patch together, from snippets you hear,
That blanket on which everything become clear."

"If you hear something horrid, you must not react
For it may be a test of your trust and your tact;
The more that he trusts you, the more he might say
And give hints about what he is up to away."

"Wise words, Mr Holmes," Kenneth Pines then declared,
"And it might be as well if you got good and scared.
In a setting of fear, all your senses will thrive -
When I used to climb mountains, fear kept me alive."

"Quite so!" announced Porter, who'd got to his feet,
"This would seem like a quite nasty fellow to meet
If one ever had crossed him." Then said, with a shiver,
"We don't want Mrs Tully found dead in the river."

"Well, has anyone else heard of anything strange?
Anyone who has had an unusual exchange,
Or has heard or has seen or has read since we last
Discussed menace in this, our Metropolis, vast?"

Lady Margaret stood up and, as she took the floor,
She glanced off to her left to make sure that the door
To their room was secure for, what she had to say,
She'd assure that, within the Tower, would stay.

"There is something I sense, though it's only a feeling,
That all through my husband's Department is wheeling
Something of significance – though, what, I don't know
But, whatever it is, I have noticed it grow."

"More than usual, Sir Humphrey is preoccupied
With events which have left him somewhat mortified.
Of course, he would never discuss these with me
But they play on his mind and they won't let him be."

"There've been many meetings with colleagues at night
And sometimes he's emerged with a face showing fright
About something he's learned. It's a worry to me
But, in these circumstances, I must let him be."

"With me, he will not discuss matters of State.
Though he's perfectly right no to do so, debate
About something that's brewing is certainly rife
And it's quite taken over political life."

"The Army and the Navy are in this, as well,
Although who's been attending, I really can't tell;
But some uniformed men, in our parlour, I've seen -
They were not there for trifles - their manner was keen."

"And, some other wives, too, mention something awry
With their husbands' behaviour but cannot say why
Such disruption to Whitehall's composure occurred,
Why into such action its tenants were spurred."

"At our recent soirée, I served tea by the pail
While attempting to get some discretion to fail
And to loosen some lips, get reserve to uncoil,
Then get hints on the source of the current turmoil."

"I tried serving sherry, although some preferred gin;
No too much, though, for quite an unspeakable din
Could occur – there'd be anarchy as a result
And no gossip at all, only raucous tumult."

"They're not shrinking violets, these ladies of State;
With most things of importance, they're quite up to date;
But I couldn't find one who had much she could say,
Not one who might give any secrets away."

"That is very unusual, I must report,
So the matter cannot be the usual sort
Of political nonsense, their lips had been tightened -
So, something quite dire has got their men frightened."

Williams added, *"For banks which are able to hold*
In their vaults, stacked as bullion, reserves of Gold,
A directive has come from a Hall very White
That security should be reviewed at each site."

"There was no reason given, just orders to act
If directives came through to report the exact
Mass of Gold being held – the entire amount -
Not from the bank's records - by actual count."

"By actual count! Not just as documented!
This Whitehall directive is unprecedented
And is cause for concern. Are we under attack
From within or without? Is the outlook that black?"

"We have notified Richards, someone we can trust
With transport of our bullion, that, whenever we must
Move substantial amounts of our treasure, he might
Be prepared to help out under cover of night."

Then the two station masters, both Johnson and Blake,
Said a few special trains were on stand-by to take,
From the city, in secret, some quite precious freight
Which would be, in its nature, excessive in weight.

"Well, who might we advise and just what can we tell
To assist that somebody to act and to quell
Any trouble afoot?" Porter asked of the rest,
"Does anyone have anything to suggest?"

As Holmes rose to his feet, he would tap Watson's arm -
Perhaps seeking back-up should scorn or alarm
Follow what he'd reveal of a recent event -
Perhaps Watson's support, either one, would prevent.

"Now - Gentlemen, Ladies – what I'll say to you now
May well cause you to laugh, but bear with me, somehow,
And believe that it's true, though the facts are confused -
I am sure, when you hear them, you won't be amused."

"As you know, down to Dartmoor, I'd answered a call
To look into outrages I know would appall
The most hardened of criminals, and so I was left
To consider a person, of conscience, bereft."

"A mind quite demented, yet cunning and bright,
Had been turning the Moors into Hell every night;
I could not find a reason that such things should be
So the only fact left to consider was me."

"There were clues, quite intangible, left with each crime;
It was not what was there but what wasn't, each time;
Someone seemed to be playing a devilish game
On the Moors with my mind – this suggested a name."

"Well, you all know the name – it is one I'd not care
To have ever need utter again, but a snare
Had been set and, into it, I stepped like a fool -
The response which I got was decidedly cool."

"Well, it took me some time and the help of my friends
To accept I was wrong and, somehow, make amends
To those colleagues distressed by my utter persistence
That someone thought dead must be still in existence."

"I had fled to the countryside, hidden away
With the bees of the South Downs, that is, till the day
That John Watson, my Beacon, considered it time
To return to pursuing the agents of crime."

"And when Watson told me it was time I returned
As the bridges which led to that fiend had been burned,
I had realised that, in my mind, I was set
To come back and not utter a word of regret."

"But, upon my arrival, a note, short and taunting,
Was found on my door and its wording was haunting;
In the fight against evil, it seems I'd been tardy -
That note on the door had been signed Maurie Hardy!"

"To over-react would have been a mistake
And we both thought it prudent, for everyone's sake,
To prepare, in some detail, a plan of attack
But to first gather facts that our planning would lack."

"I then approached Porter and Denton to say
That perhaps Dr Watson might join us some day
Very soon as we had something vital to tell
This illustrious Tower, and others as well."

"Meanwhile, we considered, Lestrade, we should tell
Although Watson would do this – he knows Watson well
And would listen intently to what he would say
While he might just tell me to get out of his way."

"As fate would have had it, Dr Watson sought out
Dr Denton, a colleague, while roaming about
On his secretive foray off to Scotland Yard,
Though a fall on his hip had him limping quite hard."

"Well, Denton thought it a fortuitous gift
To have found Watson limping in pain and adrift
And sent him with a note to seek out Porter's store
Where a famous concoction would, comfort, restore."

"Denton's note contained words in our coded format
Which suggested to Porter the time had come that
Dr Watson should learn of our company, closed,
And invite him to join if he'd be so disposed."

"Scotland Yard never learned of the outrageous note;
But I call upon Watson to stand up and quote
The grave words it contained so you all may assess,
For yourselves, what the note and its contents express."

Dr Watson stood up and he read from the note
What he said was an actual verbatim quote:
"My Dear Dr Watson, when bear hunts you require,
Is it Holmes you'd profess or Maurie Hardy, Esquire?"

"Profess or Maurie Hardy", Holmes stated distinctly,
"A very strong message, though stated succinctly
By someone who knew I'd return at that time
And who knew I was ready for battling crime."

"It may well be a ruse, a bad practical joke,
But the timing and content both serve to invoke,
In my mind, most objective, suspicion of things
Of a quite dire nature – it's given me wings."

"Who'd remember that bear, the one we all shot,
And that fellow called Hardy who just up and got
Right away but who left not one definite clue
And who always would seem to escape right on cue?"

"Who'd have known I'd return when I did on that train?
Only someone with cunning enough to sustain
Complete up-to-date knowledge of each single plan
I might make. So, I ask you, just who was that man?"

"No one knew his first name nor, for certain, his last
Although Miss Abernathy, left simply aghast
By her poor father's fate and, remembering scraps,
Guessed at Lawrence or Maurie and Hardy, perhaps."

"I suggest we stay mute for a little while yet -
If there's something quite serious stirring, I'd bet
That my brother, Mycroft, would know what is in play
And might well say to me that, my hand, I should stay."

"We'd not wish to detract from the measures now set
Into play by the banks; but Gold is, don't forget
Quite secure in vaults, under guard, as approved,
But is ever so vulnerable when being moved."

"Perhaps, I'll suggest, to my brother, that he
Might consider the prospect that there might well be
Some intrepid conspirators loose in the land
Who would get our Gold mobile and then take command."

While Holmes took his seat, Porter rose and declared
His support for the action and hoped this was shared
By the Tower, en-masse, though each must raise a hand
In agreement as the group's protocol would demand.

"It would be," said Porter, *"most judicious to hold*
Off reporting to others on matters of Gold
Until Holmes can advise his contact, premiere,
Of concerns about Gold being sent anywhere."

"Holmes' brother is quite as perceptive as he
And, in all probability, understands we
All meet up as a group but does not interfere -
He would know we're effective and very sincere."

"Mycroft," declared Sherlock, *"is quite like the stone*
In the buildings of Whitehall – he sits there alone
Never seeming to move while all things come to him -
He acts only on knowledge and not on a whim."

"He may well know our work and, perhaps, all our names,
But he'd know that our group doesn't play power games;
We'd not be on record; to exposure, not prone;
For, if something works well, he will leave it alone."

Well, the Tower approved by a mass show of hands;
Holmes must now assess whether the brains in the land's
Most august corridors knew of stirrings below
In the back streets where trouble had started to grow.

THE APPROACH

Holmes and Watson got back to Two-twenty-one-B
On the stroke of midnight, their minds obviously
In some turmoil on how they ought now to proceed.
Mycroft must be sought out – at least that was agreed.

Did they dare make approaches directly or just
Send a message that Sherlock was back and he must
See his only relation, that fellow, fraternal,
And speak with him frankly on matters, infernal?

"Perhaps it would be better to go on your own
For Mycroft might not want the facts widely known
About what is afoot and what plans are in place."
Said Watson, prepared to give Sherlock some space.

"I will send him a note saying not much at all
And my not saying much will suggest that he call
And discuss any matters which ought to be aired,"
Replied Sherlock who knew they must speak unimpaired.

"Mycroft might well prefer that I be here alone
But, as you have his trust, he would likely condone
You being present to hear of the perils we face;
I suspect, though, your presence he'd firmly embrace."

"I should send the note off without further ado;
But it's well after midnight – therefore I'll have to
Wait till morning until my Irregulars wake
And can carry my message. But much is at stake!"

"No – I'll go there myself, though the hour is late;
I will go in disguise – I will not vacillate
When suggestions of war-time emergency measures
Abound like they do over threats to our treasures."

Sherlock donned a disguise – it gave Watson a chuckle -
From his hat, coat and cane to his bag's shiny buckle,
Holmes looked, every bit, the Physician gone calling
On patients in need at an hour appalling.

He crept out the back door and, when two streets away,
Gave a call to a cabbie, asleep, that he may
Be in time for a life to be saved if he hurried -
The cabbie awoke and then, off, the cab scurried.

A block and a half before Mycroft's address,
Holmes tapped on the roof saying, *"Thank you - I guess*
I'll be here for a while, so there's no need to stay."
Once paid, to the main road, the cabbie made way.

Holmes pretended to look for his patient's address
Then, at Mycroft's front door, a small button he'd press
Which would ring the new-fangled electrical bell -
How Mycroft might react, he just couldn't foretell.

A few moments went by, then a short muffled oath
Told him that some poor servant had felt rather loath
To emerge from his bed, but would rise and then dress -
The door opened a little and someone asked "*Yes?*"

"*I've a message for Mr Holmes, Senior, my man.*
It must give it to him just as soon as I can
But must do it in person – a note can't be left -
It's important – I can't risk its loss or its theft."

Mycroft heard the commotion and bumbled his way
From his bed to the stairwell and managed to say,
Looking down to the dimly lit hallway below,
"*If we're not being attacked, I just don't want to know.*"

"*Oh, it's you.*" Mycroft grumbled, "*But why the disguise?*
Watson's medical outfit's a poor compromise;
But it's late and you're here and I'm now out of bed
And I see that, to here, you have hastily sped."

"*This isn't John Watson's,*" was Sherlock's reply,
"*And I did come in haste but I thought I would try*
To look less like a sleuth acting furtive and quick
And more like a doctor attending the sick."

With a yawn, Mycroft said, "*The next time you should try*
Even harder - your waistcoat has been sent awry
By a misaligned button – it's easy to see -
Though it might fool a felon, it doesn't fool me."

"I need to meet with you – it's urgent, extremely."
Sherlock said, saying also, *"It might be unseemly*
For John Watson and I to go barging along
To your office in Whitehall – it could be quite wrong."

"I don't wish to send signals that I'm on the job
For, if I were to do that, I'd probably rob,
From myself and from you, the prospect to retain
Secrecy in a matter I need to explain."

"I believe that I'm under surveillance, you know,
And, at home, I've a note which I feel I must show
To someone like yourself – and there's more I must tell
Of a plot which is stirring and which we might quell."

"Brother Dear," broke in Mycroft, *"your Tower has met*
And they know of some plans for the movement, I'd bet,
Of some matter, quite yellow and shiny and bright,
Sometime in the future, one very dark night."

"There's not much that escapes me, my eyes get around,
My ears I keep keen, my nose close to the ground;
One particular eye saw, attached to your door,
A provocative note by an old woman, poor."

"You don't think I was fooled by each nasty report
In the tabloid newspapers – they'll always distort
The most innocent fact to a story, insane -
Their outlook is mischievous, never urbane."

"So, a keen weather eye, I have kept on your digs
And had someone go down to the Moors when those pigs,
Or those sheep, or whatever, had dragged you once more
To the wastelands of Devon to settle some score."

"You insisted your former arch-enemy had
Some vendetta afoot and that, being a cad,
Never hesitated to be wilful and cruel
While he sparred with you in some insidious duel."

"It was obvious, Sherlock, that things were amiss
And, when you went seeking apiarian bliss,
I knew well that you needed some time and some space
To reclaim your composure and retake your place."

"It turned out Watson's timing was rather ideal
For, when he went to fetch you, your fervour and zeal
Were restored in full measure, your passion was back,
And you just couldn't wait to go on the attack."

"But, that name Maurie Hardy you found on the note
Is a name that somebody deliberately wrote
To get you to react, self-esteem to unnerve,
To unsettle your cunning detective reserve."

"You did not take the bait but embarked on a plan
And, from that, I knew that this remarkable man
And his steadfast companion would be on the scent
Of the forces of evil and would not relent."

"The old woman was later discretely detained
And my operatives, in due course, ascertained
She'd been given the note and some pins and was told
To pin it on your door if she would be so bold."

"It was given to her by some toff in a Pub
And he claimed to know Sherlock from some fancy club
And he gave her a Shilling – she said that the bloke,
On an old friend, was playing a practical joke."

Sherlock took a deep breath and he stated *"Some joke!"*
It nearly caused me and John Watson to choke
When we saw what was written and also by whom -
It was quite like a ghostly foretelling of doom."

"Who knows if it was he whom I had long presumed
To have died in those Falls, or someone who'd assumed
His identity later? Perhaps it's a fact
That somebody would want me to over-react."

"You're being openly goaded by someone, I fear."
Declared Mycroft who added, *"I'd say, Brother Dear,*
That you're someone somebody wants out of the way
For something upcoming – sometime - any day."

"Well, perhaps," began Sherlock, *"but I'll tell you now*
Of what colleagues of mine have been hearing and how
Several facts which might appear quite unrelated,
When looked at together have me quite fixated."

"Quite so!" exclaimed Mycroft, *"Your dazzling Tower,*
Although not official, has substantial power
To gather all manner of data diverse
On characters wicked and rather perverse."

"I have known about you and your friends, all along,
And your well-meaning work but, do not get me wrong,
To obstruct you, I wouldn't, to stop you, I shan't -
You will see things I cannot and hear things I can't."

"I suspected that might be the case, Brother Mine;
To detect and report is our single guideline."
Replied Sherlock, relieved by his brother's approval
And happy he'd not want the Tower's removal.

"We're aware of some stirrings in matters of State
Which are causing concern as they seem to relate
To some organisation by uniformed men
In an area, somewhere, quite near to Big Ben."

"There is talk about value in metallic form
Which is clearly unusual, not quite the norm;
And if need for a transfer, somebody might deem,
Our railways could readily cope, it would seem."

"Our docks had been quiet, that is, up till now
When a man who, some time ago, caused quite a row
Had been seen hanging 'round – he does not act alone
But is simply a dog sniffing after a bone."

"But a dog with a powerful master, I'd say,
For the same nasty fellow was seen underway
Seeking out foreign toughs and throwing 'round cash
While deporting himself with some pretentious dash."

"What connects all these factors, I really don't know
But so many unusual things go to show
Me that something is brewing, something very large,
So I'm here to report to the fellow in charge."

"I don't think that your note was a practical joke
But an item intended, from you, to provoke
A relapse to your state just before all those bees."
Said Mycroft, *"A state of being down on your knees."*

"There is one more thing which you now need to hear,"
Sherlock said, *"though it may be a little unclear,*
It's that Watson once sprung to defend my good name
From attacks by somebody who'd bring me to shame."

58

"Professor James Moriarty, it seems, had a brother
Who wrote to the papers and signed as no other
Than James Moriarty - a Colonel, he claimed -
At his brother's defence he apparently aimed."

"Two brothers called James? Well, that cannot be so.
Though it might be a error made while on the go
By a busy typesetter – they read in reverse
Sometimes in conditions extremely adverse."

"That could possibly be," Mycroft said, resisting
Agreement, *"but editors, ever insisting,*
Are generally careful with what they issue
And will double-check letters in case people sue."

"If it was a mistake, as seems probable now,
Then whoever had made it had realised how
Such a error would undermine any contention
If it, to the Public, was brought to attention."

"So, as you hadn't noticed the gaffe at the time,
It would seem that this Colonel or brother-in-crime
Or whoever had made the mistake had decided
To say no more about it lest he be derided."

"That seems very likely," Sherlock then agreed,
"Watson told me that not one more letter, indeed,
Had been seen in the papers from that time to this.
But had they been written by my nemesis?"

Mycroft thought about this for moment, remote,
And then said, *"Of that letter and also the note,*
We will proceed assuming it was the Professor
And was not, as supposed, some mocking successor."

"If we work on that basis, though we may be wrong,
We'll know what to expect or, at least, have a strong
Sense of what sort of evil the fellow might plan -
If we can out-guess him, we might get our man."

"If this fellow is trying to act 'the Professor',
He will act, with no doubt, as though his predecessor
Has come back from the dead after such a long while
And will proceed to taunt you with rancorous guile."

"So, for now, you must act like you've taken the bait
And appear to lie low but, in fact, lay in wait
For the moment he steps from the dark to the light
And then we'll come down on him with all of our might."

"On those matters you mentioned, I can't comment yet,
But must check with my agents, some whom you have met,
And my colleagues in Whitehall, and then we shall meet;
Meanwhile, appear downcast locked in Baker Street."

Sherlock made his farewells and then, out on the street,
He would walk to the main road while hoping he'd meet
A quite different cabbie than earlier met
But, if that couldn't be so, he'd not get upset.

He had his disguise though there was a good chance
That his earlier cabbie had been in a trance
At that hour of night and would not be aware
Of the dress or intention of any one fare.

It had been a long day and a much longer night
And a different cabbie was quite a delight
So he clambered on into the Hansom and groped
With a head full of ideas as, home, the cab loped.

In reverse of his outward excursion, Sherlock
Made his way back to Baker Street just as the clock
In the hall sounded Four and, two steps at a time,
He bounded upstairs for some slumber sublime.

That slumber was not, as his mind was on fire,
As sublime as the weary Great Sleuth would desire
And he tossed and he turned and then capitulated -
He'd resort to his pipe as his mind postulated.

In a ritual honed to perfection, he lit
Up his pipe while, right back in his seat, he would sit
And draw forth, from the burning tobacco, the way
To that place in his mind to where tired thoughts stray.

He would sit there till morning, just barely awake,
For his mind wouldn't let him forget that, at stake,
Was the safety of millions, both people and pounds -
He tried hard to keep all his thoughts within bounds.

He dozed off about dawn but he roused at the sound
Of John Watson, refreshed, to his breakfast, bound
Who, surprised to find Holmes half asleep at first light,
Said "*My senses deduce that you've been up all night.*"

With a wide gaping yawn, Sherlock said, "*Quite astute -
All your senses are clearly quite keenly acute
But, when we are both ready and you have been fed,
I will tell you the reason I've not been to bed.*"

"*You must also eat, Holmes – as a medical man
I insist that you breakfast as soon as you can
For we'll need all our strength for the trials ahead.*"
John Watson insisted, "*At least eat some bread.*"

"I will do as you say, though it's coffee I need
At this moment." said Sherlock, "There will be, indeed,
Many trials ahead for ourselves and our friends
Before this new threat to our great city ends."

THE SLEUTHS

Mrs Hudson then knocked on the door as on cue
And then entered and Watson could hardly subdue
His great appetite, rampant – the man wasn't meek -
One might think that he hadn't been fed for a week.

"Bless you, Mrs Hudson – you've quite saved my life -
You are quite the best cook, that is, after my wife
Who'll be wondering whether I'll ever come home -
She might well lay a frying pan over my dome."

"But she does understand that I must be on call
For my patients, as well as my friend doing all
That he can to keep crime in this city at bay -
None-the-less, when I see her, there'll be Hell to pay."

"Poor woman," replied Mrs Hudson, *"you do not*
Quite appreciate just what a treasure you've got.
There are very few wives who'd put up with a man
Who runs off chasing felons whenever he can."

"You men do not know just what worry you cause -
You go out when you like and you never once pause
To think what your wife feels left at home all alone -
It's something I feel I could never condone."

"I'd be frantic with fear if my husband went fighting
Those violent forces – you think it's exciting
To face any danger from what might be called
The vile works of the Devil – I would be appalled."

Mrs Hudson had struck a quite discordant note
On a highly tensed Watson. He said, *"It's remote*
That I am indispensible much of the time,
But I feel it's my duty to help conquer crime."

"You're right, Mrs Hudson, but could I desert
A good friend such as Holmes? I just couldn't revert
To that lacklustre fellow I'd been in the past."
Declared Watson, *"I don't know how long I would last."*

Holmes said, *"You're my Beacon, my bright guiding light*
And, if you didn't shine, I don't know how I might
Ever solve any crime, avert catastrophe."
Watson countered, *"You always do fine without me."*

"I am just there to help as a Doctor and friend
And you know, with my life, I would always defend
You against all attacks, but I always seem tied
Like a dog to a fence and should feel satisfied."

"Mrs Hudson sees clearly my place in the scheme;
We have often seen danger, at times quite extreme
So, perhaps, I should rethink what's owed to my wife
And place her needs first in my danger-filled life."

"I am torn between duties – three ways, you must know.
There's my medical practice, at times rather slow,
And my marriage to Mary – I can't let her down -
But if I would desert you, I'm shamed around town."

"There are two other duties I owe and I'll say
That the one which I owe to my country, this day
And for all days that follow, I'll honour till death
And I'll speak as a patriot with every breath."

"The other duty is that owed to myself -
I will not be the one who would sit on some shelf
Like an ornament, useless, while others take all
Of the risks which emerge when they hear duty call."

"Some may think me a bumbling fool, if they like,
But this fool would advance to the walls with a pike
And a musket and sword to defend this great land -
It would not need to ask me nor, ever, demand."

"Mrs Hudson, I'm sorry, I've no appetite
For the food you've prepared – I cannot eat a bite.
I'll return to my wife – she might need me today
And, should she insist, I'll no more go away."

Watson picked up a few private things that he needed,
His medical bag, hat and coat, and proceeded
To walk out the doorway and down the stairwell;
It seemed like he'd entered a personal hell.

Sherlock said, *"Mrs Hudson, we must let him be.*
I'm afraid that some people, especially me,
Will at times show our friend less respect than is due
And dismiss his opinions – I fear this is true."

"He'll return when he's ready – the time must be right
For the man to return and to rejoin the fight;
All thoughts to run after him, I must subdue -
This time Sherlock Holmes, it seems, hasn't a clue."

"*Do you think he'll return?*" Mrs Hudson enquired.
Sherlock answered, "*I'm not sure what will be required*
To get our friend back where he's needed the most
Which, till minutes ago, he considered his post."

"*Just consider the man and way his mind's built -*
He's been raised to accept any burden of guilt.
With his great sense of duty, we made him feel small
And I don't really know if he'll come back at all."

"*But I must still go on although Watson has gone*
And I don't have my Beacon which faithfully shone
In the darkest of times and which lit up my way,
For great evil may fall upon us any day."

"*Now, with Watson away, perhaps not to return,*
There will be midnight oil in barrels to burn
As I mull over problems, go chasing up clues,
Chasing villains and felons of various hues."

Mrs Hudson broke in, "*If I may be so bold,*
And I know that my comments were much like a scold,
Dr Watson's the type who will stand by your side
But, being ignored, he just will not abide."

"*So, maybe you should now take a good inward look*
And discover, within you, whatever it took
To cause Watson to speak of himself as some dog
Who gets tied to a fence while, the action, you hog."

"*Direct, Mrs Hudson, but also quite right.*"
Holmes admitted, though rather unsure how he might
Fix the problem, "*I'll often close up when I think*
And this led my friend Watson right up to the brink."

"But I must be off now, there is work to be done
Even though I admit that it needs more than one
Set of eyes for the task. Still, I must persevere
For the agents of evil are gathering here."

He poured out his coffee - two cups he would drain -
Ate two pieces of toast, just enough to sustain
Him throughout a full day. Though he needed to sleep,
He'd dare not – he'd appointments with evil to keep.

In the meantime, John Watson returned home to find
That his patient wife, Mary, incredibly kind,
Was up and was breakfasting all on her own -
She looked up with a start – she was quite overthrown.

"You're back! I thought you'd be gone for a day,
Maybe more," Mary said with a tone of dismay.
"I thought I would have the whole house to myself -
Don't come moping around like some sad little elf."

"I thought I'd be welcome," he said to his wife,
"I have finally pulled myself out of that life
Chasing felons down back lanes and over the moors -
As you've often said to me, I should work indoors."

Mary said, *"Well, ignore me – you usually do*
Any time Sherlock calls and he says he has to
Go off chasing some crook the Police cannot catch
Or go foiling some caper that's ready to hatch."

"That is all over now - I have mended my ways
And will be a physician the rest of my days
And be home to assist you however I might."
Vowed Watson, *"I'll be here from morning to night."*

Mary pondered a bit and said, *"Do you want toast?*
There's not much in the larder of which I might boast
But I could get some porridge on stewing, My Dear,
But I just ate the last of the bacon, I fear."

Watson first had his toast and then, after a while,
Mary's warm lumpy porridge he ate with a smile
And declared that he'd focus on healing the sick
And not go chasing after some crooks with a stick.

Mary gave him a look he did not understand.
She would, as a rule, give her John a demand
To get out from under her feet – *"You're a pest*
And you should be out doing those things you do best."

Watson settled into his lounge chair and he read
The entire newspaper then toasted some bread
Which he buttered profusely and then added jam
As his Mary looked on, then he heard a door slam.

The day went on by and the Doctor saw three
Slightly sick geriatrics but charged them no fee
As they didn't have money but wanted to chat -
Mary said she was hiding their old welcome mat.

Mary said *"You're not interested in such a life -*
You are only content when you're out facing strife
With Sherlock and other assorted crime fighters
Chasing murderers, robbers and other such blighters."

"You're a medical doctor, a good one, I know
But, for doctors, there are many streams and they flow
In quite different ways – yours is not the calm brook
But the torrent which rages – for turmoil, you look"

"When you're gone, I do miss you, but cannot abide
All your moping and pining when you're stuck inside;
You were never someone to be kept within bounds -
You need to be out chasing game with the hounds."

"You're a positive asset – that, Sherlock well knows,
But the man gets obsessed – few emotions he shows.
So, be gone with you, Man, this just isn't your post -
It's home, but it's not where you're needed the most."

"That's what Sherlock might say. Have I acted the fool?
Could I ever go back? Is my temper now cool?"
Watson thought to himself then, to Mary, declared,
"Well, I suppose, to return, I might be prepared."

That evening found Watson back in his old chair
In his bachelor lodgings, the Baker Street lair;
He was waiting for Holmes in that strange atmosphere -
Holmes greeted him warmly with *"Watson, you're here!"*

Watson stuttered, *"It's Mary -I get in her way*
It would seem, and that lady had, this very day,
Given me a few withering 'it's my house' looks,
And said I should go out and catch a few crooks."

"I don't know if I'm wanted, or welcome, indeed,
But, Holmes, I must tell you, I am of a breed
Who can handle the truth and can keep his mouth shut
But, to be overlooked gets me right in the gut."

"Are we partners, or not? If it's 'yes', I am back
But, if it is 'no', then I'll just get my pack
And try to rebuild a Practice now in tatters -
If that can't be done, well, then, nothing much matters."

"Well, you matter to me and it's partners in full
From now on, and I will not charge in like a bull
In a china shop, Watson, until we've conferred,"
Declared Sherlock, *"I do know how much I have erred."*

"Just talk to me Holmes -share your thinking with me;
I really think that, at this stage, I could be
Of considerable help – I am not a buffoon -"
Said Watson, insistent, *"I could be a boon."*

"That you are!" agreed Sherlock, *"A godsend, no less!*
Without you in my fight against crime, I confess,
That, behind my back, firmly, my right arm is tied.
For my faults, I am sorry – I'm quite mortified."

Watson's victory, he knew, would be one of degree
But, for now, he was happy that Holmes would agree
To include him in planning and keep him informed -
For some time, at least, Sherlock would be transformed.

"So, you do suspect threats from those disparate clues -
All those definite sightings and vague residues
Of some overheard gossip and beer-laden chatter,
Odd railway chit-chat and dock workers' natter?"

"At this time, I'm inclined to do more than suspect -
There is something afoot that I truly expect
Will be massive in scale, gigantic in scope."
Sherlock said, *"And with you back, I know I can cope."*

"We should meet with Mycroft just as soon as we can
And go over the facts and see what type of plan
That his agents, official, have put into play -
It would be a mistake if we got in their way."

"When you'd returned home and were sorting your mind
And mine, too, it would seem, if that's not too unkind,
I knew that, new methods, I'd have to devise,
But I pressed on alone, although still in disguise."

"I took what sleep I could, though you know I'll exist
On a few precious hours and often subsist
On those few tiny morsels of food that I need
To keep body with soul so that I can proceed."

"I did not want all London to learn of my actions
So I had Mrs Hudson cause little distractions
By turning the lamps in our rooms off and on -
As a willing campaigner, she's my paragon."

"She knew that I needed to make my escape
From the rear in disguise, trying so hard to ape
The antics of a drunkard, while she made it look
Just as if I was home and was reading a book."

"I spent time in a corner down in Tully's Pub -
For all manner of felon, the place is a hub
And a hive of activity, second to none,
From the level of plotting I saw getting done."

"That fellow was there, looking quite out of place -
It was Percy the Ponce and I saw, on his face
Which I recognised from the description Jakes gave,
An expression which told me his dealings were grave."

"I was there for two hours – I acted the drunk;
I had ordered a bottle and spilled it and stunk
Like the floor of a brewery – folks left me alone -
The king of the drunkards slumped down on his throne."

"But I listened to Percy the Ponce and I learned
That somebody he worked for apparently yearned
To have, working for him, a few foreign types who
Did not mind very much what they might have to do."

"The fact they were foreign, these types he recruited,
Suggested, to me, that they well might be suited
To actions involving sedition and treason,
I really can't find a more plausible reason."

"These fellows, all foreign, would not have been loyal
To our country nor even that Personage, Royal,
So, whatever they did, they'd just see as a job
To be done by a rather unscrupulous mob."

"In due course, Mrs Tully said, 'be on your way
If you're not buying drinks then you just cannot stay -
I've got good paying customers looking to sit
And they won't sit with you so, your seat, you must quit!'"

"This, of course, was arranged early on in that night
As I needed to leave without risking a fight
Over something inane, so she gave me the heave
At the time I had told her I wanted to leave."

"As you know, I've locations spread all over town
Where I often retreat to and also set down
To change into disguises so I may appear
Out in public without, my detection, to fear."

"So I changed from a drunkard - again, I would be
The good doctor attending a patient when he
Had been summoned to help in a sudden attack
Of some malady, on this night, freezing and black."

"*I went 'round to Pall Mall, to confer with my brother*
On matters concerning what could be another
Quite imminent threat to our people and land;
But, of course, you know much of the problem at hand."

"*He had not much to offer beyond what we knew*
And had told me before on those matters which drew
Me to speak with him urgently after we'd met
With the Tower that night which you'll never forget."

"*However, Mycroft can be cagey and sly*
And he'll give one a hint and might never say why;
He confers with the highest we have in this land
But he can't always talk – that, we must understand."

"*He will put things in riddles and, even, in jokes;*
Though he'll say very little unless it provokes
One to taking some action he cannot discuss -
Even if it's illegal, he won't make a fuss."

"*We spoke for a while, then he stretched in his chair*
And said, 'Sherlock, you know, Isaac Newton showed flair
By removing our Standard of Silver, so old,
And we'd be in a pickle if we lost our Gold!'."

"*We most certainly would,*" I agreed with a grin,
"*Perhaps someone should check if there's any left in*
Those unbreachable vaults and ensure it's secure -
To lose one single ingot, we could not endure."

"*Well, I took this to mean that he thought there might be*
Some attack on the Gold and that I, that is, we
Should investigate further, then meet and advise
If the Gold should be moved, or that plan be revised."

72

"We discussed the prospect that, as so much Gold
Would be quite hard to hide, then some other plot, bold,
Might be waiting to hatch – something quite diabolic -
Whatever, it wasn't some underworld frolic."

"What if," I then asked, *"enough Gold disappeared*
Long enough to give doubt to economies geared
To that dominant currency which it supported?
Would trade based on Sterling become quite contorted?"

"It most certainly would," agreed Mycroft, *"so we*
In the highest of circles in Whitehall would be
Most desirous of not having someone suggest
Such a threat might be coming – not even in jest!"

THE DISCUSSION

"So, what do we do next?" Watson asked of his friend,
"Did your brother Mycroft, in some way, recommend
Some direction to follow, some method to use?
Are we looking, in fact, for a fast-burning fuse?"

"I gather," said Holmes, *"the fuse hasn't been lit*
But is being prepared as, right here, we both sit.
We must find out what's needed to move all that Gold,
What's required, for so much, to handle and hold."

"We'll contact both Williams and Richards, post-haste;
Time is of the essence – we have none to waste;
We must find how much Gold's to be moved, also how,
Perhaps when and by whom, and we must do this now."

"We would need, if the Gold's to be moved on a train,
To know where it might go and where, putting it plain,
Someone with a great knowledge of every railway,
Might divert such a train and then hide it away."

"Just the very idea of that Gold being moved
Is a notion of which Mycroft has disapproved
For if just one small part of this action being done
Was revealed, the secret comes badly undone."

"If the world sees that Britain's in fear of its Gold,
The resulting furore would bring panic, untold,
And might well cause our Pound to collapse in a heap.
Were that ever to happen, Britain would go cheap."

"But, before it's put onto a specialty train,
The Gold must be transferred, with a great deal of strain,
Via wagon, in secret, by crews we can trust -
To be sure of our people is simply a must."

"The first part suggests Williams, our man at the Bank
Who might well be the fellow the nation should thank
For his sensitive ears and his diligent ways
Making sure that not one single Gold ingot strays."

"The second part points right to Richards and Co.
Whom the Bank trusts with Gold when it's needed to go
In complete secrecy, quite secure and sound -
More reliable transport could never be found."

"So, where in the chain might be found the weak link?
Where, in our armour, the vulnerable chink
Which might well be the focus of any assault
Once the Gold leaves the safety of any bank vault?"

"In the bank? In the street? At the station? Perhaps?
How can any such project be kept under wraps
From the Public at large? Everyone on the street
Will be able to see – it would not be discreet."

In Threadneedle Street, Banker Williams was sought;
He told them that things were much as they had thought
And that he wasn't happy to move Gold about
In such quantities, massive – *"The word must get out."*

"But I don't have a say, though I think that I should
For I know what's involved more that anyone could;
Such a secret could never be kept over time."
Williams added, *"We risk a most monstrous crime."*

"It might well take a week to move all of that Gold -
There is only so much that a wagon can hold;
And if too many wagons are seen near the Bank,
We'll be in for, I fear, a most devilish prank."

They sought out John Richards who said much the same.
He could handle the regular transfers, but blame
Would not be on his head if something went amiss -
He thought moving such quantities would be remiss.

"I have only three wagons for transporting Gold -
I would normally need only one, but we're told
There might be quite large transfers at some future date."
Declared Richards, *"These may exceed maximum rate."*

"The transfers would have to be secret, I'm told;
As if anyone interested in transfers of Gold
Wouldn't notice such movements – it's foolish to think
That somebody would not hear an ingot go 'clink'."

"What's our Government thinking? Or is it at all?
If an underpaid clerk learns of this, he might call
On a friend and discuss such things over a brew.
If that happens, we may find ourselves in the stew."

"We cannot keep this secret, so why try at all
When the Gold, at the moment, is safe behind wall
And iron bar, underground, where it cannot be grabbed -
In the open, some part of it well might be nabbed."

"Well, Watson," said Holmes, *"we must now be prepared*
To entrap any plotters and have them ensnared
Well before any movement of bullion commences,
Though nobody's committed the least of offences."

"Officialdom cannot just move in and arrest
Anyone it suspects – these fiends will have the best,
Most unprincipled lawyers that cash can provide -
They'd be freed within hours, not safely inside."

"But a State of Emergency might be the way
To get them off the streets long enough to delay
Any plan to disrupt any movement of Gold."
Queried Watson, desirous of actions quite bold.

But Sherlock replied, *"There's a great need to keep*
The entire thing secret and not let a peep
To the wide world of commerce slip past any lips -
There's a high price to pay for the smallest of slips."

"To declare an Emergency sends up a flare
And shouts loud to the world that it should be aware
There's an imminent threat to the base of our Pound
And it's dangerous keeping our Gold underground."

"The Gold would be safe but not where it should be
For it's placed in some danger each single time we
Move just one single ingot – but can we keep count
When thousands get mobile – the dangers just mount."

"But why is the Gold to be transferred at all?
Surely much better ways must exist to forestall
Any threat to our bullion stored where it should stay."
Watson mused, *"And what is the threat, anyway?"*

*"Exactly, "*said Sherlock, *"no one's said a thing*
On why action is needed and why we'd need bring
In the Army and Navy. Whatever's in play,
No one knows or, perhaps, is forbidden to say."

"We must surely be told of what threat we all face
If, the villains who planned it, we're able to trace.
Cannot Mycroft convince those in power to tell?"
Pondered Watson, *"Surely we need to know that as well."*

"No one's likely to try to steal Gold from the vaults.
And these villains, for all their felonious faults,
Are not stupid – they know of the minimal chance
Of escape, loaded down – they'd see that in a glance."

"Dr Watson, I thank you; I'd focussed on how
We'd watch over the Gold while en-route, although now
You have brought, to my notice, the crux of the matter."
Holmes stated, *"You've caused my distractions to shatter."*

"John Watson, I'll tell you – I've told you before
That, though my mind is a well-catalogued store
Of diverse information on all sorts of crimes,
I need someone to light up a beacon sometimes."

"My mind was at sea trying hard not to sink -
So much water around me that I couldn't think
Beyond staying afloat, washed by great waves galore,
When a Beacon lit up and it lead me to shore."

"If I've ever discounted your thoughts, I am forced
To declare that such thinking from me's now divorced
And will never return, for you are my White Knight,
My reliable Beacon, my great Guiding Light."

"Now, steady on, Holmes, don't get carried away."
John Watson, embarrassed, then heard himself say;
"It is just common sense there might be such a plot."
Holmes replied, *"It is sense although, common, it's not."*

"Mycroft had mentioned this, but I was overtaken
By plans for the movement of Gold, but you've shaken
Me out of my stupor – our focus, and his,
Should be why all that Gold can't just stay where it is."

"Before we do more searching, Mycroft we must ask
Why the country must undertake so great a task.
What is it that's got all Whitehall in a panic?
Why do Peers of the Realm show behaviour so manic?"

"I will send him a note, all encoded, so he
Will know now is the time that he must meet with me
And yourself, my dear Watson, so then he'll acquaint
Us with what's going on without further restraint."

Within a short time, this same note had been sent
And, precisely at ten, Holmes and Watson both went
To meet up at Pall Mall with Mycroft to be told
Just why Britain was forced to move all of that Gold.

Mycroft looked very weary, or worried, Holmes thought;
"There is knowledge we need and I think that you ought
To tell us what's afoot, why the Gold must be moved."
Holmes insisted, *"I do not care who's disapproved."*

"My hands had been bound and my tongue tied in knots
But I wanted to tell you the scope of the plots
We'd uncovered." said Mycroft, his hands on his flanks,
"There's an agent, explosive, which threatens our banks."

"Such an agent should be apprehended forthwith!"
Declared Sherlock, *"Just tell me his name isn't Smith*
Or something so common he'd be hard to find."
Mycroft said, *"He's an agent of different kind."*

"Nitroglycerine, Sherlock, if you want his name -
An insidious agent who's quite hard to tame
Let alone to control – with the smallest of hits
He'll explode and blow anything near him to bits."

"A chemical agent! Well, why didn't you say?"
Sherlock stated, a little annoyed at the way
That his brother had toyed with his little mistake
When he knew there was so much in London at stake.

"Forgive me, Dear Brother, I couldn't resist.
It was just a release from my days which consist
Of continued reports of great danger, impending."
Explained Mycroft, *"They just seem to be never-ending."*

"I can see," declared Watson, *"you're under great stress;*
I have seen and have felt this before, I confess,
Going into a battle when everyone knows
That some men will succumb to both bullets and blows."

"If you don't feel the danger and show any fear,
Then you are of the type I'd not wish to be near.
Confucius said that quite a long time ago
And I think, in our time, we should say it, also."

"Such fear sharpens the wits, energises the mind,
And, the means to meet danger, it helps us to find;
Ask an old soldier how, when in battle, he fared,
He'll say getting active got him through being scared."

"But some comic relief does no one any harm,
And, in fact, has been shown, many times, to disarm
The effects of a stranglehold placed on the mind
When one faces a foe of implacable kind."

"Quite so, Dr Watson! I do need release
From the evils which taunt me and seem not to cease
But, in fact, have intensified in these past days."
Mycroft freely admitted, *"On my mind it plays."*

"Between duty I owe to authority, high,
And my own full assessment of danger that's nigh
And the way that I feel that this ought to be faced,
I've been left with my mind just a little displaced."

"But, Watson and Holmes, as a capable team,
Can do things of which types like myself only dream,
And go places without the restrictions of rules,
More or less, while ignoring official schedules."

"That we can," agreed Sherlock, *"and certainly will*
Any time that we feel a particular skill,
Although strange and unorthodox, might help to quell
Any trouble that's brewing and sound its death-knell."

"Nitroglycerine, Mycroft, is not to be found
In a shop on a shelf, so we must look around
For its source, or someone who can have it prepared -
This agent, if loosed, will leave nobody spared."

"Miners use it to blow massive holes in the ground
But, since Alfred Nobel found out how to compound
It with adsorbent fillers, the stuff has been quite
Safe and easy to handle and called Dynamite."

"Both our Army and Navy use it to propel
Cannon shells after mixing it in a vessel
With guncotton and sticky petroleum base
To yield Cordite which, then, they can safely encase."

"Few will cart it about, for it's like to explode
In an untempered form and an unadsorbed mode
At the slightest sharp jolt – it is freely admitted
That transport is generally never permitted."

"Information I have would quite likely suggest
That the stuff would be made in pure form on request
And transported where-ever it might be deployed."
Declared Mycroft, bewildered, *"This has me destroyed."*

"Well, it isn't so easy to make up the stuff."
The Great Sleuth then protested, his voice a bit gruff
And his mind ticking over, *"It's not like some cake*
One might mix up a bit and then proceed to bake."

"To prepare it, one needs to have vitriol, fuming,
Aqua fortis, as well, but that's only assuming
One has all the skills and the means to mix acid
Which can't be, in any way, labelled as placid."

"One also needs glycerine extracted from fat
Added into a rather hot rendering vat -
This stuff isn't dangerous until it gets mixed
Carefully with the acids with which it is fixed."

"All parts of the process are risky, extremely
And, therefore, processors have to be supremely
Adept at the chemical methods required -
A chemist, experienced, would be desired."

"Perhaps it's a ruse or perhaps it is not.
Perhaps it's a quite clever decoy we've got
On our hands and there's some other plan underway -
More data is needed before I can say."

"We must know what is real and what game is in play
And if we are being played like a salmon which may
Strike quite hard at a bait but discover a hook -
There are fishermen prowling the banks of our brook."

"If, indeed, Moriarty's behind what we know
Is a devilish plot which might threaten to blow
Up the Gold or the vaults or the banks or whatever,
We are up against someone both ruthless and clever."

"But what of that Colonel called James Moriarty?
Is he brother or just some nefarious party?
And I must admit that, with one thing and another,
I've failed to consider the man's younger brother."

"Younger brother? You mean there's another to find?
Is this fellow that Colonel who'd quite lost his mind
And had signed off as 'James'?" queried Watson, aghast,
"Is he moulded the same way his brother's been cast?"

Sherlock said, "*I can't say but I'm tending to think*
That he well might lead us to that unknown weak link.
Two brothers, it seems, are confused about names
But I'm triply baffled if this one's called James!"

"*There is nothing suggesting this fellow's involved*
But, however, at this point, he can't be absolved
From some link to the threat of impending disaster -
The man is, or has been, a railway station master."

"*Three brothers or two or just one only-child?*
The question is starting to drive me quite wild.
So, I think we should check out this train station one
And hope he can help bring his brother undone."

THE COLONELS

At this point, Sherlock Holmes was determined to act
In a way which would not negatively impact
On his need to keep up the continued pretence
Of retreat and reflection and public absence.

So far, every excursion he'd taken at night
And he felt fairly confident that he well might
Be considered to be, by the agents of crime,
Keeping out of the picture at this present time.

He would need to maintain this illusion at length
While applying, in secret, his unequalled strength
In that reasoned deduction for which he was famed
While he searched for the source of an evil untamed.

He had promised inclusion for Watson, his friend.
He had given his word and he, now, would not bend
One iota of angle, not one small degree,
From that grave undertaking, that solemn decree.

He would need all the help he could get to maintain
An anonymous presence so he could refrain
From alerting the underworld of his intent
To behave like a bloodhound and get on the scent.

Watson said he would need a decoy of his own
To maintain the illusion which, so far, had shown
Him to be idle at home; he might think to replace
Mrs Hudson with Denton - this task he'd embrace.

Next morning, John Watson made Denton aware
Of the points of the matter while taking great care
Not to say all he knew – that would be indiscreet;
He knew Denton would jump at the task with both feet.

Without hesitation, Dr Denton declared
That, to man Baker Street, he was fully prepared.
For as long as it took, he would take the Sleuth's place
And, the absence of Sherlock, nobody would trace.

He was due for a break from his practice and he
Could arrange for a medical colleague to be
Put on call or in place to attend to each need
For attention from patients so Holmes could proceed.

Holmes returned to his Baker Street lair in disguise
By a tortuous path which he thought rather wise
If some criminal agent kept watch on who came
To the home of his brother of government fame.

At the time, just a few were alert to the plan
To uncover the plot and to locate the man
Who had caused an alarm to be quietly raised
Though the actual threat had not yet been appraised.

Sherlock now would be free to investigate who
Was about causing trouble by delving into
All the facts that he had and the hints of a crime
Which was set to occur in a very short time.

On that station master, Moriarty, they'd check
For it may be that, up to the nape of his neck,
He was implicated with his brother's misdeeds -
They must stop any outrage before it proceeds.

Watson said he would try to discern what he could
Of this fellow – he thought railway companies should
Have some record of who is employed or has ceased
That employment by choice or by being released.

He suggested to Sherlock that Jakes was the man
Who might get all the keepers of records to scan
The details of employees, both present and past;
For this, he had presence and expertise, vast.

Sherlock duly agreed and so Watson set out
To make contact with Jakes and to tell him about
The suspicions they held on this station master -
Speed would be of the essence to stall disaster.

Jakes agreed and made contact as only he might -
His determined demeanour and manner, forthright,
Would have clerks searching records for fear of his wrath -
It would take a brave man to steer Jakes from his path.

Some companies could be contacted forthwith.
Moriarty just wasn't a name such as Smith
And should quickly be found after Jakes would persuade
All those keepers of files that a search should be made.

Not all companies' records were quickly brought forth
As some held all their records and such way up north;
But they had to be asked so Jakes called upon friends
From the Force to say that Scotland Yard recommends.

Enquiries performed within London would yield
Little useful knowledge but, from further afield,
Just one sole single hint of the man they had sought
Would appear and was not quite as everyone thought.

The man, the younger Moriarty, was found
But, it seemed that his mind had been rated unsound -
He'd been judged as a risk to the Public at large
For, at folks, sword in hand, he'd occasionally charge.

This was not station-masterly conduct and, so,
To a secure asylum he was made to go
At Her Majesty's pleasure – the man was insane
And was held in a building considered humane.

Overnight, Jakes would travel to have questions posed
To the man or his doctors, although he supposed
He would not get an answer which made any sense,
But he'd try as the danger was truly immense.

It would take him no time to locate where this man
Was incarcerated and he described the plan,
Though in terms very general, to doctors concerned -
They told him of the mind of the fellow, interned.

He'd return without wasting a moment of time
For he had information he considered prime
To relate to the Sleuths – it might help to make sense
Of a situation which was getting quite tense.

He could use that new-fangled telephone thing
But he just wasn't sure how to make the thing ring
Or if people could listen to what he might say -
He would use what he knew was a much safer way.

So a telegraph message to Watson was sent
Saying Jakes would arrive and it was his intent
Not to wait for a moment in telling his news
He had gleaned from the doctors in his interviews.

Watson stood on platform awaiting the train
Bringing Jakes back to London – the wait was a strain
But he felt there'd be news of a favourable sort
When Jakes could deliver his welcome report.

In due time, the train bringing Jakes came to stop
And Watson saw Jakes, from an open door, hop
To the platform and greet him and say, *"We must catch
The first Hansom we see – I have news to despatch."*

*"I've a four-wheeler waiting along in the street
Holding Holmes and another with whom we'll now meet.
You'll find Holmes in disguise – he's a doctor today."*
Replied Watson as, quickly, he whisked Jakes away.

Down the street the pair marched at a bustling pace
Till they met the four-wheeler and looked on the face
Of a man with a beard and a small pince-nez set
On a prominent nose. *"This is Holmes."* Jakes would bet.

Holmes said, "*Get in, the both of you, Watson and Jakes.*
We have very fast horses and very poor brakes.
It's Richard's man Fenton who's driving this cart
So we're safe and, to Whitehall, it's now we must start."

"*Jakes, meet Mycroft Holmes, he's my brother and he*
Is as quite as important as one man can be.
Tell us all you have learned – we are eager to hear.
Is the man whom you sought anyone we should fear?"

"*I know of your brother, we've met in the past.*"
Declared Jakes, out of breath but in London, at last.
"*Good to meet you again, Mr Holmes. But I must*
Catch my breath and report – we're secure, I trust."

"*Having heard from my contacts the man had gone mad,*
I embarked to the North where, to say, I am glad,
That I found the man quickly, at least where he's kept -
It's a very sad place and a man could have wept."

"*Billingshaven, it's called – it's an old country seat*
Where the squires called Billings once went to retreat
From the world - until fortune had failed to shine -
Now their riches are really no better than mine."

"*An asylum, they call it, a prison no less*
For the poor wretched souls with minds under duress.
It has gardens and grounds rather grand to enjoy
But a need for strong bars, also guards, to employ."

"*It emerged,*" Jakes reported, "*an uncle returned*
From a battle in which he'd been terribly burned
And succumbed to his injuries after one year -
This uncle had held his young nephew quite dear."

"This uncle, it seems, had no time for the one
We assumed, at the Reichenbach Falls, was undone
When he plummeted downward right into the void
Like, a somewhat ironical, spent asteroid."

"He bequeathed his possessions to one he preferred
And, from what was related and what was inferred,
This nephew, a little unsound since a child,
Donned the uniform, running 'round manic and wild."

"More and more, the mad episodes had people scared
And the passengers said they would not be prepared
To step onto the platform whenever he dressed
As his much-revered uncle - they were not impressed."

"Well, in time he lashed out with his sword at a guard
On an incoming train, swinging ever so hard
Till the sword firmly lodged in the door's solid wood -
He was utterly mad, it was then understood."

"This had been near the time of his brother's demise
And it seems he decided he ought to advise
Several papers of how good his brother had been
And to sully his name, Sherlock Holmes had been keen."

"But he signed as his uncle, that Colonel called James.
This, of course, was the source of confusion with names.
We might have heard more but the man was confined
For his sake and for others' –his exit declined."

"He marches around in his uniform giving
Out orders to others - at least he is living
A life of some sort, though, of course, he's unarmed
And the railway passengers don't get alarmed."

"His doctors told me of the intriguing case
Of the man and his family, some brilliant, some base;
Of inherited brilliance coupled, no less,
With a touch of insanity hard to repress."

"The man's elder brother was brilliant but bad;
He became a professor but hated that lad
Who was simple but likeable - traits he abhorred -
But was, by the uncle, just simply adored."

"This uncle, called James, had a grandfather, daft,
Who had thrown his own mother headfirst down a shaft.
James stood up at Sebastopol waving a gun
And the Russian artillerymen had some fun."

"They blasted the fellow and all of his men
From their well-hidden trenches and stopped only when
There were none left to kill, though the Colonel survived.
Some said it was a shame he was ever revived."

"He was burnt, he was mad, and eventually died;
'Most everyone cheered though his young nephew cried.
It's a very strange seed their ancestors have sown -
The Mad Moriarty's, that's how they are known."

"This explains a great deal," declared Sherlock to Jakes,
"And, from our dilemma, a factor, it takes.
We now know there can be only one Moriarty
To fear, if alive, not a family party."

"It's a shadow we've chased, but it's one we could not
Have ignored for it might have led us to the plot
Or whatever it is which requires our Gold
To be moved from the vaults to locations untold."

"It also reduces the scope of the plot
For I think that, of now, just as likely as not,
We are confined to London, perhaps just outside -
Our luck may be changing – fortune's on our side."

"It doesn't directly add much to the count
Of what we can now say of the total amount
Of what we can call 'fact'," Mycroft quietly mused,
"But one of our problems is surely defused."

"It has taken two days to find he's not involved;
The results are quite good, but it still leaves unsolved
Many mysteries, urgent, we have to explore."
Said Watson concerned that he might have done more.

"Quite so," replied Sherlock, *"but now we can focus*
Our eyes on our great metropolitan locus
And not be distracted by mysteries beyond
Greater London – I think we have time to respond."

"There's more," added Jakes, *"for we checked in the files*
In the dungeons of Billingshaven where the piles
Of documentation were held on each man -
They would tell me what only such full records can."

"He's incurable, that's what the doctors all think;
But he's harmless enough if the man's made to drink
Down some calming concoction 'most every day -
When he does, all his demons are made go away."

"Up till one month ago, no one sought out the fellow
Although their concoction had kept the man mellow.
He had only one visit, this poor addled man -
A friend of the family - Colonel Moran."

THE SHOCK

"Moran – he's in gaol – he deserved to be hanged!"
Yelled Holmes, as his fist to his open palm banged.
*"The man is possessed of such devilish skills
That, if he were set free, we should head for the hills."*

*"I could never believe that he would be released -
There are so many people he had left deceased
That he ought to stay locked behind bars in a cage
So nobody falls foul of his devilish rage."*

*"We must check if the man was somehow liberated
Or if he, as I hope, is still incarcerated.
If he's in, he'll be harmless, though evil and sly;
If he's out, then - By Thunder - I'll want to know why!"*

*"You'll remember, My Friends, it was he who had shot
At me when I escaped from that Reichenbach plot;
He's a rather dead shot with an air-gun, you see,
But too great a distance allowed me to flee."*

*"He's a gambler, of sorts, but the odds he will trim
By resorting to cheating a likely victim
Who expects it's a gentleman dealing the cards
But is really a cheat with some helpful blaggards."*

*"His credentials, impressive, his history, grand,
Meant that gentlemen's clubs anywhere in the land
Would hold open their doors to admit the man in -
He'd play cards with the best and he'd generally win."*

*"He'd make sure that he lost just enough to convince
Any gambling partner, from high noble prince
To Northumbrian merchant, that he was sincere
And played only for sport in a grand atmosphere."*

"He'd get some into debt but he'd soften the blow
By extending his credit, and then they would know
That he was a good type, generous to a fault,
And would, thus, find his way into many a vault."

"But his evil intentions, his devilish side,
Were found out and, exposure, he could not abide;
To avoid his expulsion for not playing fair,
He murdered the Honourable Ronald Adair."

"It was Mrs Adair who would plead for the life
Of this fiend to be spared – opposition was rife
But her pleading succeeded, the sentence to hang
Was commuted to life, to be served with his gang."

"She did not see the death of this murderer served
Anyone – and his hanging would leave her unnerved
And unable to grieve for her son as she ought;
So, clemency, unto this mad fiend, she had sought."

"Moriarty, in him, had a valuable asset -
He'd hunt with his master like some skilful basset
Who flushes the game from where it is concealed -
Between hound and the master, it's fate is then sealed."

"We must find if he's still behind bars or at large
Because, if he is free, he is liable to charge
At the ones who have beaten him at his own game -
Though he's not Moriarty, his evil's the same."

"We'll drop Mycroft off close to Whitehall and when
He is back in his office we'll hurry and then
Get Lestrade at the Yard, or someone, to confirm
That Moran, in his prison, continues to squirm."

After Mycroft took leave of his friends, a loud shout
From the cabbie was heard as the cab came about
And a crack of the whip had the horse running hard
Till they got to the street just outside Scotland Yard.

As they saw Scotland Yard come, at last, into view
Holmes threw open the door – he and Watson then flew
From the carriage like rabbits pursued by a hound;
Their feet never seemed to have contacted ground.

Jakes followed along at a much slower pace;
He could not match the much younger pair in the race
To locate and request, of Lestrade, his assistance
And hopefully not meet with any resistance.

Lestrade saw them coming and stepped out to meet
The illustrious pair running hard in the street
Well ahead of Dan Jakes who was starting to puff -
Lestrade was quite cheerful and not a bit gruff.

Lestrade said, *"Mycroft rang and he made me aware*
Of the facts of the matter ... well, all he might dare,
By means of that magic device, telephonic -
Slow down before Jakes takes a fit, catatonic."

"I've been on to the prison – your man is still there,"
And he will not be able to go anywhere
For the rest of his evil and miserable life;
But he did have a visit last June from his wife."

"The telephone, Holmes - you should get one installed
So, instead of the telegraph, you could be called
By those types who might feel they've a need to consult
A detective, of sorts, for an instant result."

"They will never catch on," declared Holmes with disdain,
"And from having one inside my home, I'd refrain.
The telegraph's really the means I prefer
And I'd not, to a ringing bell, ever defer."

"But what of the knocking on doors at midnight?"
Enquired Watson, displaying his eager delight
At the thought his old friend becoming connected
Directly, *"From that, you cannot be protected."*

"But a message in writing is better, instead
Of hysterical yelling right into my head."
Holmes declared, while waiting for Jakes to arrive -
Jakes looked for a while like he wouldn't survive.

"When I talk to a client, it's better for me
Face to face as expressions are able to be
All observed, for so much is expressed by the face
And a lie, very often, is easy to trace."

"But, a message in writing requires contemplation.
The mind must achieve at least some relaxation
So that facts can be listed, suggestions proposed;
And emotion is rarely, if ever, enclosed."

"Enough!" then retorted Lestrade, *"It's Moran*
We are here to discuss and not how people can
Talk directly together, though miles apart -
We've work we must do so we should make a start."

"I will start," offered Holmes, *"by declaring Moran*
To have been, by desire, an unmarried man.
And, unless he's been wedded while locked in his cell,
This wife is someone we must look for as well."

"She's made numerous visits, the Warden confirmed."
Lestrade added, while Watson uncomfortably squirmed
At the thought of another unknown in the plot,
"So she'd be an accomplice, as likely as not."

"A messenger, probably - someone to carry
His orders to others. He'd not likely marry
And probably couldn't – it isn't allowed,
Or so I am led to believe." Holmes avowed.

"So, one mystery's solved but two rise in its place."
Sherlock said, with a look of concern on his face.
"Moriarty the younger is safe behind bars,
But we seem inundated with criminal czars."

"Just who is this woman who visits Moran?
And who, may I ask, is the mystery man
Who takes time to go visiting young Moriarty?
We are up against some rather devious party."

No sooner had Sherlock expressed his desire
To discover the facts, a new message quite dire
Was rushed into Lestrade– he went white in the face -
"This is the last straw – this is just a disgrace."

"This says that a check of his cell has revealed
That Moran has absconded from where he was sealed
For the good of Society, and it could be
He'd been gone some time – it's a catastrophe."

"He's out!" Holmes erupted, *"When did he escape*
And how did he do it? It's starting to shape
Up like he is our villain, our foul mastermind,
Though I thought, for such planning, he wasn't the kind."

To the telephone desk, Lestrade ran with great haste
And requested, forthwith – there was no time to waste -
To contact Warden Harris who'd sent the report
That Moran had absconded – his temper was short.

To the Warden he shouted, "*My God! How did he*
Ever come to escape and just how could it be
He'd been gone without his being missed for some time?
And just how long was that? This mistake is a crime."

"*And a crime it might be,*" the Warden would admit,
"*I have asked for the records and checked every bit*
And each comment recorded on checks we have done -
It seems we have three missing felons, not one."

"*I've detained several guards – one's admitted his guilt*
But, right now, I'll not cry over milk that's been spilt -
They've been gone for a while but, how long, I can't tell;
Each one had been marked as present in his cell."

"*I don't know what to say; this will mean my career,*
Not to mention the course of great evil they'll steer
When they act, as they will, in their criminal ways -
I fear we are in for some worrying days."

"*I will question the prisoners for what they know*
And will telephone you with the facts which might show
Any hint of a scheme that the trio had planned;
Though I am, at this moment, a bit undermanned."

"*But, from some information which has been produced,*
It appears that a few of my guards were induced
To provide them with clothes and to help them escape.
A nasty conspiracy's starting to shape."

"I don't know if my guards had been bribed or, instead,
Had succumbed to a threat of some action they'd dread
On themselves or their families – more will emerge -
To tell all, there is one who is right on the verge."

"But two who escaped had been part of the gang
Which had been apprehended but not sent to hang
As had some of those felons who had been employed
By him who we thought Sherlock Holmes had destroyed."

"I can't say, at this time, that Moran has been kept
Behind bars all the time for, as everyone slept,
He might well have slipped out of his cell to attend
To some business, outside, with the help of a friend."

"And that friend, I suspect, was a guard he'd induced
To assist him, somehow, in a way that produced
The illusion that he was still locked in his cell -
The guard would have helped Moran return, as well."

"Could it be that Moran was in league, as before,
With that evil Professor that Sherlock Holmes swore
Had been killed, so he thought, but had then reappeared
To rebuild that empire which Sherlock Holmes feared."

"Does anyone know if the man is alive
And is likely, one day, to abruptly arrive
And upset the decorum this land now enjoys
By one of his deadly and devious ploys?"

Jakes jumped in, "We don't know, but we do think it wise
To proceed as though chasing someone in the guise
Of that devious fellow – the man we all fear.
Is he dead or alive? Well, that just isn't clear."

"Things suggest he's alive, though that might be a ruse
That someone has devised to distress and confuse
Mr Holmes, both to ridicule him and divert
His attention from things to which he'd be alert."

"Both revenge and reward for a type such as he
Who has, ever so often, been beaten by me
In those masterful ploys which his mind has contrived."
Agreed Sherlock, *"Perhaps Moriarty survived."*

"We must let whomsoever is planning the crime
We suspect will occur in a very short time
Keep believing I'm out of the picture, forlorn
In my Baker Street rooms from which I won't be torn."

Lestrade added that, *"Mycroft was, too, of that view;*
And Sherlock, in disguise, should keep eyes on the crew
Which that horrible Percy the Ponce had recruited -
Sherlock, he declared, would be admirably suited."

"Warden Harris has not, to the Public, announced
That Moran is at large, but he has quickly pounced
On the guards and prevented such news, in or out
Of the prison, to leak – it will not get about."

Dr Watson, confused, and somewhat overwrought
Posed a question no one, up to that time, had thought
To ask of anybody of official standing,
"When Moran jumps the wall, where would he be landing?"

"I thought you all knew," Lestrade quickly responded,
"The prison from where this Moran has absconded
Is a place to avoid – that is, if you are smart -
It's way out on Dartmoor – it's called the Old Dart."

THE PLOY

"On Dartmoor – My God! Could Moran be the one
Behind all of those crimes and those outrages done
On the folks on the Moors?" Watson asked, in alarm,
"Was it him with the bear that had done so much harm?"

"That seems very unlikely," Holmes said to his friend,
"A bear needs a handler, a strong one to bend
The instincts of a beast such as we had to fight -
But to handle the handler, Moran just well might."

"I suspect that the handler is probably dead
For Moran wouldn't need him and, therefore instead
Of him risking discovery, would have the man killed -
There'd always be someone to do what he willed."

"So, this glimmer of light is a quite vital clue -
If Moran is assumed to be guilty, he's due
For a very rude shock for he hasn't the wit
Moriarty would have, though some facts clearly fit."

"He's resourceful and cunning, courageous, corrupt;
He's the sort of a man who might like to disrupt
And upset all our banks, our financial affairs,
And make off with the loot while we make our repairs."

"But, of course, it could be that he isn't the one
Who is planning whatever's about to be done;
His planning is thorough for any one deed
But, for something so complex, he might not succeed."

"There could still be a much larger brain behind this,
And I'm thinking out loud that my old nemesis
Might have laid down a plan quite some time in the past
But had died well before any die could be cast."

"That might well be so," Watson said to his friend,
"But what might have occurred that's so awful to send
All those government types into spasms of fear?
Mycroft, I'd suggest, hasn't made this quite clear."

"For the Army and Navy to be on alert,
There is something afoot, though it's clearly covert
In its nature and of some considerable size -
The Gold in our banks may not be the main prize."

"Watson, my Beacon, you may well be right.
With your practical thinking, you've now shone a light
On a region of darkness," the Great Sleuth declared,
"Our nation's great leaders were truly quite scared."

"To our nation, itself, there may well be a threat.
Nothing less could have had them break out in a sweat
Quite as cold as reported. Is war imminent?
If so, what type of act are we here to prevent?"

"Getting facts from my brother and those in cahoots
Within Whitehall's like pulling teeth out by the roots;
They will tell you so much - getting more is a task
Though, to get anything, you must know what to ask."

"If we knew what to ask, we would not need his help!"
Watson yelled, his voice raised an octave to yelp
Like a hound, quite excited, but also irate,
"He must tell what he knows before it is too late!"

"I agree," concurred Jakes, *"before anything blows*
We must get Mycroft Holmes to tell us what he knows.
A bloodhound needs a scent it can follow, but we
Seem beset by some herrings, as red as can be."

Lestrade joined in too, but was eager to say
That, *"We've only a few facts to go on today
And, apart from Moran on the run from the Dart,
There's not much of a crime for enquiries to start."*

*"There are hints by the score about trouble ahead;
We have old crooks appearing and someone who's dead
Making plans to do something, and Gold getting set
To be moved somewhere else, but no fish in our net."*

*"We've a government minister going berserk
Like some fish with a hook in its mouth when a jerk
On the line has caused it to react and to splash,
But we can't see the fisherman making him thrash?"*

*"I assume it's not France that's about to invade
And it would take a great deal for you to persuade
Me that Germany's armies are set to embark -
So, what is this danger so urgent and stark?"*

*"Scotland yard is not actually up to the task
Of repelling invaders, so I suggest ask
Your illustrious brother just what is in play
Or find somebody else he can play with today."*

*"I'm as loyal as any and have a commission
To uphold the Law but do not have permission
To roam as you do, Sherlock Holmes – that's a fact;
So just get me some details and then I can act."*

*"Get Mycroft by the scruff of the neck, if you must,
And shake him till he rattles and all of that rust
That's built up over years of just sitting around
All comes loose and falls down to collect on the ground."*

"Then shake him again till his tongue starts to rattle
And tell him to forego that frivolous prattle
And tell you the facts of the matter at hand -
Do not ask him politely, resolutely demand!"

"We may have no time for finesse or for tact
So get him to take chances, himself, and to act
As if we were at war and to not expect thanks -
Before I was a copper, I stood in the ranks."

"Did you, indeed! That's something I'd not known."
Uttered Sherlock, astounded, *"This matter's now grown*
To the point where some action, decisive, is needed.
Your suggestion to rattle Mycroft will be heeded."

"To Whitehall, we'll go, without further delay
And I'll collar my brother Mycroft and I'll say
That, before we go further, he must be prepared
To tell us, in full, of what's getting folks scared."

"If he will not comply, then we must call his bluff -
Tell him that we can't take any more of this stuff
That he feeds to us, teasingly, morsel and crumb -
Trust us with all he knows and to not act so dumb."

"If he doesn't tell all, we'll retreat to our homes;
Myself back to Baker Street, Jakes to the tomes
He was reading before from his pile of books,
Watson back to Mary, Lestrade to his crooks."

"Our working on less than a need to know basis
Has led us all into an absolute stasis;
For, what we are all up against, we're in the dark
And don't know upon what tack we all should embark."

So, the four made their way back to Whitehall to see
Sherlock's brother, Mycroft - they were sure he'd be free
To receive them, en-masse, but were not sure he'd tell
All he knew of whatever, their nation, befell.

Mycroft greeted them all but was somewhat annoyed;
Their arrival, unheralded, all but destroyed
A quiet moment of thinking on how to proceed -
It would seem, interruptions, were all he would need.

"*We deduce,*" declared Sherlock, "*the threat to the Gold
Comes a very poor second, and what we've been told
Suggests something more sinister looming ahead
So we'd now like the truth, not some story, instead.*"

"*Moriarty's involvement's unlikely, at best;
Moran has escaped several times but could rest
Between outings quite comfortably back in his cell
With no bother from guards - they were paid not to tell.*"

"*I believe Moriarty is probably dead
But an old plan of his, with Moran at its head,
Is about to be set into action quite soon
So we'd like a few answers this fine afternoon.*"

"*So, to get to the point, there's no way to proceed
Unless you give us all of the data we need
To be fully aware of the dangers we face -
If you can't or you won't, it's back home we all trace.*"

"*Moving Gold's a precaution, that's what we assume,
And to have to move Gold anywhere, we presume
There is danger ahead; what that is, we don't know
But the doubts and the rumours are starting to grow.*"

"Take us into your confidence. What do you know
That we don't, Brother Mycroft? We need you to show
Us what we might be up against, all of us here -
The full picture of peril, the danger severe."

"You must realise, Sherlock," said Mycroft in shock,
"If I told all I knew then some others would lock
Me and all of you here in a dungeon so deep
No one else in the realm would hear one single peep."

"That's a risk you must take – we do not have the time
To sit down and discuss legal points so sublime
That they'd take several months to get you to agree
To tell us all you know." Sherlock said, *"Can't you see?"*

"If you don't tell us all – that's one hundred percent -
We'll go back to our kennels and stay off the scent
Till catastrophe strikes – what that is we don't know
But the time has arrived you must tell and must show."

Mycroft went very quiet, he'd never have thought
That he could, by his more active brother, be brought
To the point of conceding that he could be right -
He decided to do everything that he might.

"Give me just one half-hour to send off a note
Which will summon a party quite able to quote,
To your own satisfaction, the troubles we face;
Give me, Brother Sherlock, a smidgin of space."

"We'll be back in one hour, no less but no more,
And if we do not get what we need, then before
You can say Moriarty, we're all off the case."
Said Sherlock to Mycroft, *"The crooks you can chase."*

Then, without more ado, the determined group stood,
Their message delivered, for bad or for good,
And they moved from the office of Mycroft then out
To the street to mull over what might come about.

"Well, the cat's with the pigeons, I'd say, so we might
Have a walk 'round the block, for it could be tonight
That we're dropped in a dungeon in chains in the dark."
Stated Jakes, quite enjoying this dangerous lark.

"If I'm lucky, it would be the dungeons for me,"
Said Lestrade with a grimace, *"Though I'd likely be*
Sent up north or out west to walk beat on the Moors
Around Yorkshire or Devon, on foot, all outdoors."

Doctor Watson agreed but he said, *"In my case*
I'd be sent to treat patients, depraved and quite base
In their personal habits and manner of life
And who live where disease and infection is rife."

"Well, it seems that it's dungeons for you and me , Jakes,"
Declared Sherlock, *"unless we are tied to some stakes*
To await the attentions of somebody who
Likes a big blazing fire, with not much to do."

"Quite so!" bellowed Jakes, *"I could do with some heat*
For my feet are quite cold and it would be a treat
To be granted some warmth from a government man.
Are you sure, Mr Holmes, that this wasn't your plan?"

"Getting burnt at the stake? Well, that would be a way
One might get our attention and Mycroft might say
That his secrets are safer if we cannot talk."
Said Sherlock, *"So why don't we go for this walk?"*

"Jakes has said," uttered Watson, *"his feet are quite numb*
But as we, as a group, stick out like a sore thumb
To the spies of whoever is planning some crime,
I suggest we go walking in pairs at this time."

"So stop speaking of dungeons and fiery stakes
For the thought of such penalties gives me the shakes."
Dr Watson insisted, "So, *Holmes, you're with me*
And a fine pair of doctors we must seem to be."

Both Inspector Lestrade and his old colleague Jakes
Then walked on with the pace of a cab without brakes -
Just a pair of detectives, official and ex,
Off discussing a case proving very complex.

Lestrade said to Jakes, as they went on their walk,
"I can see Mycroft's problem – the man dare not talk
For, like me, he is held by officialdom's grip
Whereas someone like Sherlock can shoot from the hip."

"I know just what you mean but, at times, we've a need
To go out on a limb and to somewhat exceed
What are well defined limits in which we might act."
Replied Jakes, *"Though we must show remarkable tact."*

"I do know of your meetings with Sherlock and friends,"
Said Lestrade, *"though discussion of Towers now ends;*
We do not interfere and we never discuss
And such meetings proceed with no hint of a fuss."

"It might now be the time to meet up and compare
Any further developments, should someone care
To suggest to some others the time is now ripe
To refresh information and sort out the tripe."

"That's the difficult part," Jakes admitted, *"we must
Take whatever is said and report what we trust
To be useful titbits – we cannot report facts
For we must maintain faith with our many contacts."*

At this point, they saw Watson and Holmes going back
Toward Mycroft's Department, both right at full tack,
And decided to wait for a minute or so
Before they would return to that office, also.

Holmes admitted to Watson there was a mild risk
They'd be met by a few burly sorts who would whisk
Them away to where-ever whisked people reside -
He didn't have guarantees he could provide.

*"You know, Watson, I'm not sure what Mycroft may do.
He's my brother, of course, but is loyal to
That Department he works for, whatever it's called,
Where the fellow's, undoubtedly, firmly installed."*

Both groups, each of two, reassembled once more
And ascended the stairs to see what was in store
From the man, enigmatic, who seemed to pull strings -
They would find out what bluffing the Government brings.

Mycroft walked out to greet them, a little reserved,
And gave them a look which left all quite unnerved;
He bade them go in to his office to greet
The most eminent person they're likely to meet.

*"Now, Inspector Lestrade, Mr Holmes, Mr Jakes,
And, of course, Dr Watson, this gentleman takes
A most positive stance on a crisis most sinister,
Meet, if you will, our most gracious Prime Minister."*

THE VISITORS

With mouths wide agape, the four sleuths stood erect
And had looks on their faces which had the effect
Of displaying surprise of a type quite extreme
As they gazed on a personage fully supreme.

Before either the four or their honoured guest spoke,
Mycroft said to all present he'd like to invoke
An insistence for secret pragmatic debate
Between parties on matters which threaten the State.

The Prime Minister said, *"Gentlemen, take your seats.*
It is not every day that Holmes Primus entreats
Me to come to his office for talks of this sort -
Holmes Secundus, I offer my utmost support."

"It is difficult for me to speak out of school,
Euphemistically speaking, but only a fool
Would refuse to discuss any pertinent fact
Just as long as it's done with appropriate tact."

"I will take it for granted that all seated here
Are behaving as patriots and not as mere
Idle peddlers of gossip who wish to be thrown
Juicy titbits of hearsay to feign as their own."

"For, if that is the case, then at once I must go
From this place and impress on Holmes Primus that no
Information, restricted, be given away
To unauthorised persons till some later day."

Lestrade got to his feet and he looked at his friends
And he said, *"I assure you, each here comprehends*
What you're saying, in full, and no doubt each agrees
That he will not divulge what he hears or he sees."

"*I hold a commission from our Gracious Queen;*
Dr Watson has held one, and action has seen;
Likewise Mr Jakes, ex-Detective Inspector,
While Sherlock has been a most valuable vector."

"*On my oath, I can vouch for all three of my friends*
And will sign any documentation which ends
In us being permitted to hear what's induced
This immense wall of secrecy to be produced."

"*Mycroft has his ways as, also, have we all*
To collect information but now there's a call
To forget, for the moment, our different ways -
What we hear, we assure you, between us, it stays."

Four documents, out from a drawer, Mycroft took
And he said to his visitors, "*Please take a look*
At these documents and, that is if you agree,
Please sign them so that, to speak with you, I'm free."

"*It sets out, for those who would know secrets of State,*
What's permitted as well as the probable fate
Of one who has agreed but who breaks with that trust -
When you've given your word, then, to keep it, you must."

"*To abandon that trust could be taken as treason*
So don't give us here in Whitehall any reason
To regret the faith which, in you, has been placed -
If you do, and you run, you know you will be traced."

"*The penalties can be extremely severe*
So I beg that you all in this office adhere
To the absolute letter of what you have signed -
Our prisons, for comfort, have not been designed."

"This, I say as my duty – I know that all here
Are of excellent character and are sincere
In requesting more knowledge to meet any threat -
When told of the penalties, most people sweat."

The four looked at each other and nodded a sign
To the other inferring they all would align
Themselves with the requirements set by the State -
Then each read, in detail, without more debate.

One by one, each would rise and then take pen in hand
And declare and then sign that each did understand
The content of the document which they had read,
Well aware of the penalties which they might dread.

Mycroft witnessed each signature, then gave a bow
To the Premier person while saying that *"Now,*
Some disquieting matters we may impart
But we need one more person so that we may start."

"I hear someone approaching by way of the stairs
So we might rearrange our collection of chairs
To a circle so that we may speak in a way
Which is certain to not let a word get away."

"It's Sir Humphrey, I'm sure - I had asked him to come."
The Prime Minister stated, *"For he has what some*
Might describe as a finger placed right on the pulse
Of the trouble that's making so many convulse."

"A pulse quite erratic, I'm tempted to say."
Uttered Mycroft, *"A patient might well pass away*
With the heartbeat Sir Humphrey's been feeling of late -
Let us pray that our nation won't meet with that fate."

"Our patient is healthy." Sherlock butted in,
*"It's excited and just cannot wait to begin
To do battle with any foe, foreign or not,
Which has set into play a most devious plot."*

"Well said!" the Prime Minister yelled with some pride,
*"Holmes Secundus means facing our fears will provide
Us with knowledge and courage to meet any test -
When she's facing some threat, Britain is at her best."*

*"Here's Sir Humphrey, so Mycroft, if you'd be so kind,
You might make introductions and perhaps remind
Everyone in the room that, though speech here is free,
Details can't be spread through the nation with glee."*

*"Sir Humphrey, come in and sit down among friends;
The Prime Minister's here and he duly commends
You to speak on that matter quite freely to all."*
Mycroft said to the Minister out in the hall.

"I had gotten his note but am somewhat confused."
Said the Minister, wary and rather bemused.
*"Prime Minister, greetings! Two Holmes I can see;
One Senior, one Junior – though, unknown, are three."*

The Four rose, as did Mycroft who made introductions.
*"Please meet Dr Watson – he helps with deductions
When Sherlock goes forth on his secret forays
And reports in the Press of his marvellous ways."*

"Please to meet you, Sir Humphrey," the Doctor replied,
*"But I fear Mycroft Holmes might have somehow implied
That my function is really much more than it is -
I help Sherlock out but the method is his."*

Sir Humphrey replied, "*Well, it is a great pleasure*
To meet you, although I do feel that your measure
Is more than you state – I subscribe to the Strand -
Both Detective and Doctor, a partnership grand."

"*But, never, have I met Sherlock Holmes in the flesh,*
So to speak, though our worlds will, at times, intermesh
But not come into contact. My wife's big fan
And she follows your exploits whenever she can."

Holmes accepted the Minister's hand knowing well
That he knew Lady Margaret who often would tell
Of her husband's behaviour and that of his friends -
To be ignorant of her, he'd have to pretend.

"*Mr Holmes, I'm so glad that we've finally met -*
To the bottom of things, I do hope we can get."
Holmes replied, "*Sir, the honour is truly for me*
And, working with Mycroft, I'll finally be."

"*Quite so,*" said the Minister, "*now, who have we here?*
Do the looks on those faces display a severe
Type of outlook, or even some strained indignation?
No, I think that I see dogged determination."

Mycroft spoke up and said to the Minister, "*Pray,*
Permit me to present two fine men who well may
Represent what is meant by integrity, true -
By saying this, I hope I might give each his due."

"*Late of Scotland Yard, is this gentleman, here,*
Who retains, even now, the distinct atmosphere
Of the force of the Law - so, may I please present
Ex-Inspector Jakes, a man most eminent"

"Standing by him's a colleague, an important cog
In our working machinery, one likely to clog
Up our gaols were he to be given his head -
Meet Inspector Lestrade whom all criminals dread."

Sir Humphrey gave each a handshake, firm and strong,
As if saying to all that, as they now belong
To a circle of secrets, they'd have his trust now -
Then, to the Prime Minister, gave a curt bow.

Introductions completed, the door would be shut
So no one would ever suspect anything but
A most commonplace meeting on matters mundane
Though the actual topic verged on the insane.

"Sir Humphrey, I'd ask," the Prime Minister started,
"That you'd outline, to all, what our agents imparted
Of troubling rumours quite hard to dissolve -
Both Berlin and Paris these rumours involve."

Sir Humphrey sat up, then leaned back on his chair,
Ran the fingers of both hands through locks of his hair
While taking a breath very long and quite deep -
"What I'll tell you has caused me the loss of much sleep."

"To Embassies German and French have been sold
Several documents stating that enemies, old,
Have conspired with us to commence an attack
On the other by means of a stab in the back."

"Now, naturally, these two nations must take
Such a notion quite seriously and would make
Every effort they could to determine how much
Could be taken as fact, therefore danger, as such."

114

"We, ourselves, have received documents much the same
As received by Berlin and Paris in some game
Someone seems to be playing for very high stakes -
It could be world war if they're not shown as fakes."

"We all distrust each other to varying extents
But these documents serve to extend any rents
In that delicate fabric called peace we enjoy -
We must find who's behind this most dangerous ploy."

"Should we send our Fleet's ships any wartime alert
It would send, to all parties, a sign to revert
To their plans for defence, perhaps even attack -
Once that happens, there may be no way to turn back."

"Should the French be incited to make such a move
On our bases, we would obviously disapprove
And take steps to remove them, but then we would be
On our way to a war and a catastrophe."

"Our ships, at least some, would be sent to prevent
Any North Sea incursions, though this might foment
A reaction by Germany's burgeoning fleet
Which would steam from its bases, our forces to meet."

"And if Germany's Navy is threatened up north,
Then its massive land forces might all sally forth
To prop up its defences around its Empire -
This isn't an outcome which we would desire."

"And, should Germany's armies march out west and east,
Then the Russians would take quite a dim view, at least,
And be forced to take measures - their armies might clash
Should one man, overzealous, do anything rash."

"Should the Ottomans sense that the Balkans might rise
Once the Russians have moved and, perhaps, improvised
A revolt against them and the Austrians, too,
Europe then would resemble a lunatic's zoo."

"The tensions are real but a fuse has been set
In a powder keg, Gentlemen, and I can bet
That one nation or other will light up that wick
And will blow up us all unless action is quick."

"So, the plans to move Gold are precautions prepared
In advance just in case we find ourselves ensnared
In some massive hostilities brought to our shores
And would shake all our banks right down into their cores."

"But, as Mr Holmes Junior, so rightly expressed,
Any movement of Gold on that scale is confessed
To be such an endeavour it might be perceived
As resorting to panic and badly received."

"We've compounding dilemmas in front of us now.
Though we must act decisively, we must, somehow,
Prevent anyone lighting that fuse which will start
Such a war which would blow all of Europe apart."

"Diplomats can converse but the Generals will act
With an urgency mostly devoid of all tact;
When the war dogs get going they can't be called back
Till they've all tasted blood – everyone in the pack."

"That's the gist of it, Gentlemen – now you all know.
I admit that our progress has been rather slow
But we had to tread slowly and softly and not
Seem to give any credence to any such plot."

There was silence, intense, 'round that circle of chairs
Until Sherlock spoke up with, *"No one more despairs*
Of the problem we're facing, but that won't dispel
Any danger that's real, its agents repel."

"Had there formerly been any stirrings so bleak?
The South African wars caused the Kaiser to speak
In a manner belligerent – could this have been
In some manner related to threats we have seen?"

"We're assured," answered Mycroft, *"that isn't the case*
Even though Wilhelm's rantings have caused us to chase
Up an end, quite decisive, to African friction
Between us, despite his demands of eviction."

"The French tell us little but we can discern,
From that they do not, there's no cause for concern
From what could be a threat of them being attacked -
They feel they are, too, into war, being backed."

"The notes they received had been bought for a price,
Whereas those we obtained we got on the advice
Of an agent we trust who'd been told where to find
Documents of a quite diabolical kind."

"It seemed fishy enough but we had to suppose
That they could be quite genuine and, thus, impose
Stringent defensive measures – it mentioned our Gold-
The French and the Germans, of this, were not told."

"Meanwhile, we've discerned, in a round-about way,
That, for their Gold reserves, there's no movement in play
To remove them to safety – that danger's unknown -
So the only Gold put under threat is our own."

"But what of that agent we spoke of before?"
Sherlock asked of his brother, *"Do you feel there's more
Than just bluff in the rumours? I feel it's a ruse -
Nitroglycerine's just too unstable to use."*

"I must admit, Sherlock," said Mycroft, red-faced,
*"The rumours of that nasty stuff can be traced
To this office you sit in – I couldn't allow
You to find out the truth and to spoil things, somehow."*

Sherlock thought for a bit and then gave a wry smile
As his mind started pulling apart every file
That was stored in his brain-attic specially stocked -
Every drawer, every cupboard was getting unlocked.

The Prime Minister frowned, Dan Jakes was perplexed,
Sir Humphrey was dumbstruck as Sherlock's mind flexed
With incredible strength as its memory strained
To retrieve every detail till nothing remained.

"I have it!" said Sherlock, *"At least what I think
Has been bringing these nations right up to the brink.
It is clear to me, now, why I had to be led
To those Moors where red herrings to me had been fed."*

*"Information I have, I did not realise,
Would contain the sole key to a foul enterprise
Which was planned long ago but not put into play
Till the time was felt ripe at a much later day."*

*"Well, in summing things up, I can readily say
That this truly has been a most challenging day,"*
Declared Sherlock, not one little bit terrified,
"And, really, I see that our task's simplified."

THE TASK

"Simplified?" bellowed Mycroft, *"But things are a mess*
And our Government's under the utmost duress
With the threat of a war of a magnitude vast,
And you sit there amused while you should be aghast."

"I assure you, amusement is not what I feel,"
Replied Sherlock, *"but now, from this mess, we may peel*
Several layers of mystery, cleverly placed,
And uncover the devious plot we have faced."

"Mr Jakes has cleared up the confusion I felt
With an evil professor I thought had long dwelt
In a watery grave but who seemed still alive
And who would, to take vengeance, vindictively strive."

"With the rumours of war and the threats to our Gold
And escape from his prison by one very bold
Who we know had been in this professor's employ
And who would, a deep confidence, often enjoy."

"And down near the docks has been spotted someone
Who had been in the Dart and who could well have done
The leg-work for this scheming Dartmoor escapee -
He's called Percy the Ponce. Mr Jakes, you'd agree?"

"That I would, Mr Holmes, and I think we should name
His controller and tell everyone of his fame
Or his infamy, rather, and military past,"
Dan Jakes said, in agreement, *"his wickedness vast."*

"I agree," declared Sherlock, *"though we should act soon*
For he will, sensing triumph, be over the moon
With his own self-importance – he wants to succeed
Like his long dead employer – he does have that need."

"We are speaking, of course, of one Colonel Moran
Who, with military training, would know that one can
Get the Generals twitchy enough to defy
Any Government order to wait and stand-by."

"They might cancel all leave and put men on alert,
Pull the covers from field pieces and then revert
To conducting manoeuvres which, plausibly, might
Send a signal that they are expecting a fight."

"And the Admirals, when they see Generals twitch,
They, as likely as not, would get squadrons to switch
From a boring existence moored at a home station
To have boilers afire to await relocation."

"The French and the Germans have agents who see
Any change in ships' status, as also do we,
And they would, in some haste, report billowing smoke
From the funnels of warships and, action, provoke."

"Prime Minister, pray, could you have implemented
An order which would have such action prevented.
And, by personal message, perhaps, not by letter -
By yourself or, perhaps, by whom you think is better."

"Any ships put on station should now be recalled -
This would have any chance of an accident stalled
Even though it might seem to give ground to Berlin
Or to Paris – we're backing off, not giving in."

The Prime Minister spoke when Sir Humphrey advised
That Sherlock's suggestion indeed minimised
Further misunderstanding and, consequently,
Would keep peace for a while, if not permanently.

120

"Indeed, Mr Holmes, we will do as you say
And take action accordingly, without delay.
I will give orders that such acts should be prevented -
Sir Humphrey will see that they are implemented."

"I will tell them in person or, if far away,
By means telephonic, and, to all I will say
That no action be taken, no signal be sent
To suggest an attack is indeed imminent."

"Several signals in code we shall send to instruct
That all ships, newly stationed, will all now conduct
Themselves back toward home port regardless of how
Any officer feels – to this order, they'll bow."

"We must commandeer any device that we need
To convey these demands to our forces with speed;
In the meantime, I trust, we'll be after this man
Causing trouble – this infamous Colonel Moran."

"I assure you, we shall," declared Mycroft, "also
Every one of his gang and, this time, he will go
To the gallows, no matter what anyone thinks -
In that long length of hemp he won't find any chinks."

"But, Prime Minister, now, perhaps you might depart
And, to speak to your Admirals and Generals, start.
The carriage you came in is hidden away -
Both yourself and Sir Humphrey must stop war today."

"Once the Navy's recalled and Army brought down
From their forward positions, we'll inform the Crown
Of the dangers we've faced but, of course, not our Queen
Who is currently ailing - the Prince must be seen."

"At the highest of levels, we then will engage
With our neighbouring nations and defuse the rage
Which was starting to form in the military mind
And replace it with thoughts of a more peaceful kind."

With appropriate ritual deference paid
Unto those now departing, Mycroft had a staid
Look of anguish - one edged with a faint hint of hope -
With the danger explained, would the nation now cope?

Could his brother locate where this Colonel Moran
Was in hiding, and could he unravel his plan
To cause mayhem and mischief to people and Gold?
Could he stop him from doing such damage untold?

"Well, Sherlock, you have what you wanted, at last,"
Mycroft said to his brother, *"the die is now cast,*
So to speak, and I trust that you'll act in a way
That will not let our secrets go too far astray."

"It's quite unprecedented, at least in our time,
That you've gotten to speak to our Minister, Prime,
About matters of State and then had him indulge
You by telling you what he'd not wish to divulge."

"Now, the four of you here know just what is at stake
And I trust that each one of you knows he must take
Stringent steps to ensure that the secret is kept -
Detectives and Doctors, at that, are adept."

"I think I can speak for us all," Brother Mine,
"For we now have the knowledge we need to refine
Our wide search knowing war is not likely to start -
My thoughts on the matter, I now will impart."

122

"Now that order's emerging from out of the mess,
I think we can say that it is a fair guess
The 'old woman' who pinned up that note to my door
Was Moran's 'wifely' visitor out at Dartmoor."

"Your agents, Mycroft, should be trained to observe
Just a little more closely – it's bound to unnerve
The interrogators of this 'elderly lady'
That she was, in fact, ninety-nine percent shady."

"While your fellows kept watch on my Baker Street flat,
She was watching your watchers and decided that
She could pin up the note knowing she would be nabbed
But, in doing so, find out who's having her grabbed."

"Moran must have known you'd be watching my door
When I was to return from the bees and the moor.
'Poor old woman', you called her? Her finances are fine
And upon her last birthday, she turned thirty-nine."

"That's the trouble with us, most especially me,"
Declared Mycroft while almost admitting that he
Might be wrong, just a little; then said with a smile,
"We show too much compassion and not enough guile."

"But one thing we are sure of, as much as we might,
And that is that Moran thinks you're out of this fight
And are cooped up in Baker Street too scared to move
Lest you do something of which the Press won't approve."

"Too much compassion! Well, that is a giggle
You had one of his gang but your men let her wiggle
Her way out of your clutches," said Sherlock, bemused,
"The professional users, this time, had been used."

"It was Daisy the Dip – her professional name,
If I am not mistaken – the woman is game
For most anything that evil minds can conceive -
What she wants you to think is what you will perceive."

"She'll be working with Percy the Ponce, you can bet,
And as criminals go, the pair makes a fine set
Of professional felons - they stick to a plan
And they are of a sort highly prized by Moran."

"If this Percy's as wily as Daisy is smart,
Then whatever Moran, to the pair, would impart
Would be done to the letter – the pair wouldn't veer
From the well prepared path each was given to steer."

"We must seek Mrs Tully for what she has gleaned
From her Pub near the docks from the felons who leaned
On her bar telling stories which they volunteer
After drinking much more than their quota of beer."

"So, you're saying," said Mycroft, "our nation depends
On the loose tongues of felons encouraged to bend
Their much overused elbows to guzzle more grog -
It's a curious concept – my mind is agog."

"I am sure," countered Sherlock, "that many's the time
You've encountered somebody you've needed to prime
Up with alcohol before you could pump him of facts -
It's a very strong person who never reacts."

"But, back to our task – we have no time to waste
And so I will contact Mrs Tully with haste.
I'll not risk being seen, so I'll send off a note
By Irregular mail – I should stay remote."

"That will take far too long." declared Watson, at length,
"The best cabby's horse would have neither the strength
Nor the speed to make Baker Street under an hour -
We don't want Mrs Tully's hearsay to go sour."

"An Irregular would then have to get to the Pub
To deliver the message though all of the hub
And confusion of London at this time of day -
Then he'd have to return by the very same way."

"It would be after dark by the time we could act,
So, it's you or it's me who must go – that's a fact;
But, as you might be recognised, I am the one
To contact Mrs Tully – that's said and that's done!"

Sherlock spotted the signals of action impending
In Watson's demeanour – the Doctor was sending
A message to all that he was taking charge
Of this part of the battle – a soldier at large.

He would not risk the train – he did not know the way
To get to Tully's Pub – he could well go astray
Once he found himself walking in places unknown -
To this dark part of London, he'd have to be shown.

To the docklands, therefore, in a Hansom he rode,
The Doctor, this time in a messenger mode
Seeking out further details of matters which could
Cause the demise of millions if, fail, he should.

There, however, was hope that the armed forces might
Now be taken off stand-by and station, and light
May emerge from a dark situation but, still,
The evil behind things might be set to kill.

Dr Watson could not do a thing to increase
The top speed of his Hansom – and couldn't release
All the thoughts about how and of when and of who
Like his friend, Sherlock Holmes, was quite able to do.

But, his duty was clear and so it would be done
To the letter, and he never would let anyone
Get between it and him – he'd go down resolutely
Without hesitation, he knew, absolutely.

But, the task that he had did not call for heroics -
He'd avoid confrontation and stand like the stoics
Of old, hard and fast – he'd collect information
On matters concerning the fate of his nation.

On approaching his target, his cabbie was asked
To pull up a bit short – Watson tried to seem tasked
With attending a case of assault with a knife -
A common occurrence in this place of strife.

Mrs Tully, he'd summon, and ask if she had
Any more information on that Percy cad
Who seemed central to everything planned to occur -
He may not be the horseman, but he is the spur.

To an urchin, a note and three pennies he gave
Saying there were three more in his pocket he'd save
And would give to the lad when the note was delivered -
Watson looked at the folks in the street and he shivered.

Mrs Tully sent word that the Doctor should go
To a shop down the road where her friend Alfredo
Would keep him out of sight – it was there he'd pretend
That it was a deep knife wound he'd come to attend.

Alfredo was wise to the ways of his friend
And, without hesitation, his aid, would extend
To this stranger, complete, just because she had asked -
Mrs Tully, he knew, was a saint when unmasked.

Ten minutes went by and Watson thought he might
End up beaten by ten burly brutes in a fight -
A body afloat in the Thames, their hallmark;
He would like to get out of the place before dark.

But, at last, Mrs Tully appeared and said, "*Man,*
You're the last one I thought it would be, but I can
Give you some information of where, though not what -
I can tell you where Percy the Ponce likes to squat."

"*I can tell you also that, with Daisy the Dip,*
He had been away somewhere on some sort of trip.
Where they went, I don't know, but they did it by train;
When he's gone, I admit, I've no cause to complain."

"*They come and they go and they have a few friends*
They have gathered, it seems, from the filthiest ends
Of the Earth where I'd wish they'd return to post-haste -
While my patrons aren't angels, these fellows are waste."

"*These fellows are rough but not local, you know,*
And this fellow called Percy has several in tow;
Maybe six, maybe seven, I've spotted with him
And, I'll tell you, I'd not like to be their victim."

"*They speak often of railways and sometimes of ships*
And I heard someone say there is one who equips
Them with what they should need for whatever they do -
They refer to him often but do not say who."

"It's Percy who does all the talking, well...most;
And he speaks of this person like some sort of ghost.
I do not have a clue who this person might be
But, whoever it is gets referred to as 'He'."

THE SEARCH

While Watson was off on his dangerous jaunt
Seeking habitats people like Percy might haunt,
Lestrade had returned, taking Dan Jakes in tow,
Back to Scotland Yard – there was more they must know.

Lestrade said he would telephone Dartmoor to see
If more convicts were found to be out roaming free
Undetected, as Colonel Moran was discovered,
And if anyone, anywhere, had been recovered.

He would also enquire if he knew of a link
Between Percy the Ponce who had been in the clink
At the very same time that Moran had been sent
To Dartmoor – and, if so, would he care to comment.

Warden Harris could add no more onto the tally
Of convicts, absconded – he'd needed to rally
More men for the search of the entire place
To find, of Moran, any vestige or trace.

He said, *"Three men had escaped, one being Moran,*
But the other two missing included a man
Who had worked in the London Zoological Park
But was sent up for bear baiting – just as a lark."

"He'd been a prize-fighter of major prowess
And it's many a rival who's come out a mess
From the ring after taking his powerful right -
A man beaten by him is a terrible sight."

"Bertram Bennett's his name, Big Bertie to those
Who knew well not to fight him if ever he chose
To take any offence at the least little thing
That was done to the man in or out of the ring."

"Why he hadn't been missed is a mystery to me -
Such a man must be watched all the time so that he
Will not cause any trouble – he made some lives hell
And, as often as not, was confined to his cell."

"And the other?" enquired Lestrade, quite annoyed
At the great waste of time the Police had employed,
Not to mention the effort and danger they faced,
When arresting this man who must now be retraced.

Warden Harris continued, *"The other was Smith,*
First name Henry, a fellow quite talented with
Any hatchet or knife – he dismembered his wife -
An ex-butcher, the fellow was sent up for life."

"It was said at his trial his wife might have been dead
Before she had been butchered and, therefore, instead
Of a hanging for murder, the judge gave him life -
Here, the man was quite creepy but never in strife."

"I must inform Holmes," Lestrade commented, then
Insisted the Warden inform him just when
The trio had gone missing and when they'd returned,
Though he knew any bridges behind them were burned.

129

Warden Harris said he would comply, though he thought
That he could not supply that which Lestrade had sought,
But would try to his utmost to sort out the mess
Of the records – a quite hopeless task, he'd confess.

Lestrade hung up the telephone, then said to Jakes
"Back behind bars I'll have him, whatever it takes.
With his type of evil, our nation can't cope -
I've a long list of those who are due for the rope."

"A bear-baiter and butcher are loose with Moran
And have been for some time, although maybe his plan
Called for killing his helpers once Holmes took the bait -
Leaving no one alive is a true Moran trait."

"But I must advise Sherlock, or Watson at least,
That we do know who had brought that terrible beast
To the Moors when we all thought Sherlock a bit mad -
For a man such as he, such a fate would be sad."

"Well, it does have a bearing, I'm sure on this case,
For we know that Moran is the one we must chase;
It might clear Sherlock's mind of all doubt that remains -
Moran may be smart but he lacks Sherlock's brains."

Off to Baker Street, Jakes and Lestrade then commenced
Hoping soon they would have the offenders all fenced
By the agents of Law who would pounce on their prey
Which they would, to the strongest of prisons, convey.

Meanwhile, Sherlock Holmes had been doing the rounds
Of informers and gossips, not all within bounds
Of what might be called legal in manner of life,
But they would know the source of all manner of strife.

He would hear of the rumours of trains full of Gold
Which were leaving the city; how Big Ben was sold;
And how building the Tower Bridge sent London broke;
How there'll soon be no coal left and even less coke.

How London was sinking down into the mud;
How the value of money will drop with a thud;
The people he spoke to lived life on the wing -
If they weren't told the truth, they'd believe anything.

But Sherlock dare not tell them the stakes which were bid
By that felon, malignant – he must keep them hid
Till they can be negated and brought to defeat -
He must hear what folks tell him then make his retreat.

"I believe our main Gold vaults are old and are due
For refurbishment soon, so I'm forced to construe
That some Gold might be moved until that has been done."
Was the story that Sherlock would tell everyone.

"This, of course, would be done with a great deal of care
And it would be a fool who would think he might dare
Take an ingot or two from the train under guard
By both Police and Army – they'd find it quite hard."

"This is not widely known, so don't spread it around
For, if some types hear this, they'd be probably bound
To tell others about it." said Holmes knowing well
That, to all that they saw, they were certain to tell.

There were rumours aplenty, but very few facts
Upon which to rely, but there were some contacts
Who could tell of a group near the docklands with cash
Which they spent in a manner a little too rash.

"Do you know any names?" Sherlock hopefully asked
While, by this time, appearing around town unmasked,
Not disguised as a doctor but standing up tall -
A detective, outstanding, examining all.

This was no time for altered identities, for
He must question some types who would mostly abhor
Any thought of assisting officialdom's men
But who often saw Sherlock as just one of them.

They knew he had no interest in their little lives;
He would search out the evil behind them which thrives
On maintaining their misery, keeping them down,
And so could go readily all over town.

He found little more than he already knew
But did get some quite useful hints from a few
Of his regular contacts –ones who held his trust,
A commodity which, in his world, was a must.

One particular hint was of one known as Percy,
'The Ponce', they all called him, someone without mercy
When someone was with him to make him look big -
"He dresses quite smartly but he's just a pig."

"He is backed by a bruiser, a fellow called Bert
Who seems, by the size of his fists, to assert
His effective authority over his gang
Made of foreigners who will, in time, surely hang."

"But they do seem well paid and to not take offence
At how they are spoken to, ever, and hence
Might be seeing a bonus ahead to be paid -
They don't seem the type who'd be very afraid."

"Percy's seen with them all, in a group or alone,
And he speaks to each one with a menacing tone.
He's the one dishing out all the dosh to them all
But he goes, once a week, to a club in Pall Mall."

"To a club in Pall Mall? Well, he might not stand out
For he dresses quite well and he can get about
In such parts of the city unnoticed by all."
Said Sherlock, amazed at this underling's gall.

Sherlock's contact then added, *"This over-dressed louse*
Also visits someone at a Curzon Street house
Which is mostly unoccupied, so it appears,
But lights have been noticed whenever he nears."

To himself, Sherlock thought about Mycroft's address
Which was Pall Mall as well – it would be quite a mess
If this fellow, or who he had visited, knew
Of his late night-time visits and kept him in view.

"But this club," Sherlock queried, *"do you know its name?"*
Then received the reply, *"Well, no. Just the same*
It's somewhere at the west end, I'm told, of Pall Mall -
Some posh University Club, I recall."

"Moran," Sherlock thought, *"is an old Oxford man*
And a Military club would have long placed a ban
On this dishonoured officer, soundly disgraced,
But others might not have him so clearly placed."

"Was it here that Moran had been hiding since he
Had escaped from the Dart? Could it possibly be
That he'd watched all his comings and goings and kept
Both his eyes and ears open while everyone slept?"

Curzon Street was an address which few could afford
So the man must have money – there'd be a record
Of just who, on a residence, cash, had expended
But was absent for periods fairly extended.

He would seek Mycroft's help in determining who,
At least where, in that street, one might be pointed to
Such a place with someone who might never be seen
But paid cash in advance through a safe go-between.

"Do you have that address?" Sherlock asked his contact
Who replied to the Sleuth, *"As a matter of fact,
I don't know it, exactly, but on its front door
Is the name of the house – I'm told it's 'Dartmoor'."*

*"What a cheek! What a clue! Is it real or a trick?
Could Mycroft determine, and could he be quick,
Who is resident in this suggestive abode?"*
Sherlock thought to himself, trying not to explode.

Sherlock thanked his contact; a Gold coin, to him, tossed;
Made his way to the Thames which he hurriedly crossed
And then hailed a cab to be taken at speed
To Whitehall and his brother with great news, indeed.

Up the stairs to the office of Mycroft to say
That he needed more help and it must be today,
Sherlock rushed taking two steps or more at a time -
He'd tell Mycroft his neighbour's the Master of Crime.

Mycroft took the news in his stride, but he knew
That his brother and he could have been in full view
Of the one they were seeking while doing their best
To put this man, finally, under arrest.

Mycroft wrote a few notes to be acted upon
By his agents, post-haste – called them in, whereupon
He picked up his telephone, barked out a string
Of orders, explicit, to arrange everything.

"We're off, Bother Mine," he said grabbing the arm
Of his brother, *"we're off – we have need to disarm*
A felon most devious, wily and clever
If he isn't caught soon, he may well be caught, never."

"I've a message from Jakes and Lestrade to instruct
You, that is if you're seen, that you need to conduct
Yourself back to your home, to your Baker Street base,
To compare information before giving chase."

Back at Baker Street, Jakes and Lestrade had arrived
To observe Sherlock's stand-in who'd gladly contrived
To stay put and indoors while the Sleuth moved about -
Dr Denton saw Jakes and he gave out a shout.

"Jakes – is that you? Are you in on this too?
Sherlock's hopping around like a mad kangaroo
In disguise, leaving me alone manning the fort -
Of course, I was eager to lend my support."

"It's most certainly me!" declared Jakes with a grin,
"And I have someone with me and, so, to begin,
I would like you to meet an official detective,
Inspector Lestrade, a policeman effective."

"Inspector Lestrade - glad to meet you. I've read
Of your work in the papers when tracing the thread
Of obscure evidence leading to the arrest
Of the guilty." said Denton, now tired of his rest.

"I, at first, was excited to be in this den
Of detection but now, I admit, freely, when
So much time had gone by, I was hoping I might
See some action and even get in on the fight."

"There's a time we must fight and a time we must wait;
And one never should hasten to take the first bait
One might see, for one might find a hook hid within."
Lestrade said to Denton while hiding a grin.

Though Lestrade knew, quite well, that the Tower existed
And that Jakes was a member, he wisely resisted
The urge to say more until Sherlock returned;
His whole being, however, for action, had burned.

He did not know if Denton was one of that set,
Though he guessed that it would be a good each-way bet
That he probably was, otherwise why would he
Stand as sentry for Holmes, just as keen as can be.

Small talk was then made on the case, but no new
Vital facts would be shared among them till the crew
Would be fully complete – such discussion, they'd spurn.
Holmes and Watson, the group, had to wait to return.

Fifteen minutes went by and a Hansom appeared
In the street causing Denton to say, as it neared,
"One passenger, only, I see carried here.
It's Watson – for Holmes we must just persevere."

Persevere, they would do, drinking coffee in pots
Till, at last, Holmes appeared, with a brain tied in knots
Trying hard to unravel the threads of the case
Which he now might attend to, now back at his base.

As with Mycroft, a circle was formed to discuss,
In a manner, direct, and without any fuss,
All the facts of the case, both the new and the old,
On the matter of Colonel Moran and the Gold.

Watson started things off, telling all what he learned
At the pub Mrs Tully ran and how he yearned
To get out of the place just as soon as he could
But, to get information, to stay there, he would.

He said that he'd been told of how Percy had hired
A collection of foreigners, and it transpired
That he was backed up by a fellow called Bert
Who was, with his fists, a proficient expert.

Lestrade then spoke up saying that Jakes and he
Had found out that Moran could now possibly be
In cahoots with a murdering butcher called Smith
And a bear-baiting boxer that they escaped with.

Jakes added to this that the boxer was known
As Big Bertie, a fellow with fists overgrown
To the point they were hammers he used to persuade
All renegers to honour agreements they made.

Holmes listened intently, especially keen;
News of a bear-baiter and butcher were seen
To have strengthened the theory he'd taken the bait
Set by someone on Dartmoor – it was worth the wait.

When it came to his turn to share all that he knew,
He said something quite startling had come into view
Since they left Mycroft's office –and things, it appeared,
Were all coming together – the end, they had neared.

Holmes told of how Percy spent time 'round Pall Mall
And the club where, on someone, the fellow would call
And sometimes at the nearby house, eerily named -
'Dartmoor' it was called, and it got him inflamed.

"This is very suggestive, I'm sure you'd agree,
And I've left Mycroft with what I might call a free
Hand to act as he wishes – he has my support -
So, now we are waiting on Mycroft's report."

THE RUSE

"It's at times like this, Holmes, that a telephone would
Be quite handy as, without delay, Mycroft could
Speak directly with you when he's found what we need."
Lestrade said to the Sleuth who responded, *"Indeed!"*

"But, as I've said before, they're an infernal curse
On one's privacy and they're a drain on the purse.
One has no time to think, to consider what's best -
By demanding quick action, the caller's a pest."

"You're a dinosaur, Holmes, thinking that way's old-hat
And belongs with those bones, bare and ancient, seen at
The museum." Lestrade answered back, with a grin,
"They're impressive, of course, but remarkably thin."

"So, those beasts would be with us if they had invented
The telephone, which would have, somehow, prevented
Their final demise, years ago?" Holmes remarked,
"Without telephones, they, for extinction, embarked?"

*"Lestrade, you'd agree that reacting too quickly
Would cause many errors to mount up so thickly
They'd bury the truth – all facts must stay distinct.
And, Lestrade, I'm alive - those old beasts are extinct."*

*"Quite so! And I'm glad of that fact, my old friend.
Despite recent events, you need never defend
Any method you use,"* Lestrade gladly declared,
"But the telephone's getting us all quite ensnared."

*"The telegraph has, I agree, been a boon,
But the telephone will be the way, very soon,
That we speak to each other and fill in the gaps
Left in telegrams which can contain only scraps."*

Sherlock thought, then replied, *"Lestrade, how can we
Take a telephone with us to where we must be?
We would have to get messages sent without wires -
That will never occur, despite all our desires."*

*"A telegraph message will find us, somehow,
Or we will find it. We do not have to bow
To this thing which demands we surrender our time
Every time that it rings. Now, to me, that's a crime!"*

"Holmes, you're impossible." Watson declared,
*"We should use any means and should never be scared
Of these novel devices - remember those who
You had said would fly freely when shown what to do."*

*"But, no more of this banter – I hear the approach
Of what I would suspect is a four-wheeler coach.
This might well be your brother with news to impart -
It is no horseless carriage, but horses and cart."*

It was Mycroft, indeed, and the fellow had news
Of a quite vital sort – he had sent several crews
To explore Curzon Street, Moran's house to locate,
The one labelled 'Dartmoor' on front door or gate.

Out of breath after climbing the stairs at a rush,
A normally reserved Mycroft started to gush
About 'Dartmoor', the house, and its strange resident
Who, while so often gone, no one knew where he went.

"We've questioned all 'round him, with delicate tact,
And were told that the fellow had not made contact
With one single neighbour in the course of four years."
Reported Mycroft, *"We compounded their fears."*

"He has not been seen coming or going, at all,
But a smartly dressed fellow has been seen to call
In the past several months, though he lets himself in,
But no one knows his business." he said with chagrin.

"I've ten men stationed nearby, and two on a roof
Near the house, and I hope we shall soon have the proof
That this man in the house is the one we all seek -
My men are well armed – Moran will not be meek."

"But my men won't approach him – they have to report
What they see or they hear – information is short
On the lay of the house, what is hidden within -
My men are attuned to the drop of a pin."

"There are other things of which you should be aware
The first being that, with a great deal of care,
We have, in preparation, a trap to be set -
With luck, we shall soon have our man in our net."

"We've commissioned, in secret, some ingots of Lead
Painted Gold, as a ruse, to bring up to a head,
The conditions which might cause this fellow to act -
When we catch him, the debt that he owes, we'll exact."

"Also, at this moment, we're trying to find
Any plans of the house so that we are not blind
When it comes to the time when we must barge on in -
When we get these, it will be the time to begin."

"Mr Williams is ready, John Richards is primed;
We'll be acting as though everything has been timed
To the second to transfer our specialty Gold -
To be quite indiscreet, Richard's men have been told."

"The word will get 'round that the move is about
To begin – and the Gold will, of course, be brought out
From William's control into Rickety Jack's -
Some time after this, we expect the attacks."

"We'll have lookouts stationed at various stages
Along the path taken in case he engages
With Richards and his wagons before our Lead hoard
Can be brought to the train to be loaded on board."

"Moran won't be aware, and I do hope he's not,
Of the action we've taken to defuse the plot
Which would set several nations against one another -
Britain owes quite a debt to your group, Little Brother."

"To substitute Lead had been planned for some time;
From the first solid hint of a devious crime
Against all of the Gold in the vaults of our banks -
But, with war in the offing, we had to close ranks."

"That Gold-painted Lead, over several weeks,
Has been sent to the vaults so if anyone peeks
When we stage our transfer via Richards and Co.,
It would seem all the Gold from the Bank's on the go."

"From the time the fake Gold is removed from the vault,
It is subject, we're certain, to sudden assault
By a gang, hard and ruthless and led by Moran
Or that underling, Percy, a dangerous man."

"I really don't think," added Sherlock, *"they would*
Try to steal any Gold from the wagons. How could
They escape with enough for it to be worthwhile?
In our narrow streets, they'd be caught in a mile."

"No! I feel that the theft, more than likely, would come
When the train's underway – they might transfer some,
Bit by bit, when the train's left the city's precincts.
Thinking otherwise goes against all my instincts."

"But, just to be certain, we should be prepared
To face any surprise by those men who have dared
To assault Britain's banks and risk conflict, untold -
The people we face are both deadly and bold."

"But, Brother, you had not divulged this before.
This ruse using Gold-painted Lead – I deplore
That you kept it from us when we should have been told.
We were hot on the trail but were left in the cold."

"I had kept back this knowledge for fear that it may,
By a slip of the tongue, to our foes, find its way
Before I could confirm it was all in the vaults."
Mycroft sheepishly stated, *"I admit to my faults."*

"As of now, you know all – it, indeed, has been placed
In the vaults, over time – our foes would not have traced
The deliveries we made throughout twenty-one days -
The false bullion will move, but the genuine stays."

Sherlock mulled this over and he said, *"I admit,*
You were probably right to have held back that bit
Which was not then confirmed. Now, when do we begin
To move Gold, that is, Lead, for my patience is thin."

"At midnight, tomorrow, Richards has been told
That his wagons are needed to transport the Gold
To the station for loading on two special trains
Which await the instructions my office retains."

"Destinations of both are known only to me
And the fate of the Gold when it gets there will be
Divulged only when seals on a satchel are broken -
It will be written down, not a word need be spoken."

"We'll have military guards looking after this loot -
They are veterans, all, and they know how to shoot;
Their officers will try to keep them in line
But, if they have to fire, they know that is fine."

"Meanwhile, I expect we'll have news of the plans
Of that Curzon Street house– we have also made scans
Of all laneways and alleys, escape routes which may
Let our slippery eel get cleanly away."

"We have men in reserve just in case we are tricked
For, although every word of our plan has been ticked
Off as checked and rechecked, there is always a chance
That this fellow, to our chosen tune, will not dance."

"But, though we had expected there might be behind
All this talk of warfare between nations, a mind
Which was steering us to where we could never retreat -
A war all would lose – we would all taste defeat."

"We are grateful to all, though, to name you, I can't,
And to put this on record, you know that I shan't,
But we were rather blind until, to us, you came -
For, while we felt the evil, you gave it a name."

"We must now keep our nerve till things get underway -
We must wait patiently and not let a word stray
From our lips about matters about to unfold -
We'll make fools of the felons who'd fool with our Gold."

Sherlock listened, intently, then quietly quipped
As notions of action, throughout his mind, skipped,
"Indeed, Brother Mycroft, this Gold's for a fool -
When he finds it's all fool's gold, his conceit will cool."

"But evil is with us, and will always be -
Our adversary will be the worst one that we
Will encounter for decades – it will be our shame
If we now cannot thwart him, whatever his name."

"Moran, Moriarty? The second is dead
I believe, but the first operates in his stead
And has set into play this most dangerous ruse
Which even the first was reluctant to use."

"Moran, I believe, will be trying to show
That his mind, whose capacity was far below
And beneath his old Master's, is truly the best -
He would prove it by putting that plan to the test."

"He has not the conception of finesse or tact,
He is wily, of course, but I know, as a fact,
That he will obey orders if ever they're given -
But the one he'd obey, far from this world, was driven."

"So, this able Lieutenant, to Captain, aspires
And, to be the new Master of Crime, he desires;
And, although he, as Colonel, has held a Commission,
There appears, in his make-up, a glaring omission."

"That omission, of course, is he that he would refuse
To see possible faults in the methods he'd use
Or the men he has chosen – he has not the wit,
As his old Master had, to his own faults, admit."

"It's for pride that he works, not for Sterling or Gold;
Moran, I believe, wants the world to behold
A new Kingdom of Crime, and he thinks that the crown
Will be worn by whoever can bring Britain down."

"He will not need an army - he'll just use his brain
Which he thinks is superior, holding disdain
For those of mere mortals – the man fools himself -
His brain's not of a giant but might well suit an elf."

"Does he not think that people around him would see
That whatever's afoot is an evil set free
And those people would rise to protect what is theirs -
Their homes and the Kingdom, the Queen and her heirs."

"We are few in this room, but we had the resolve
To determine the source of a threat to involve
Several nations of Europe in war which would end
In disaster for all – to the jungle, descend."

With their plans set for action, to start at Midnight,
There was little to do, save for Mycroft, who might
Wait for news of the house plans he'd asked to be traced;
His men could be, then, more strategically placed.

John Richards made ready his drivers and teams,
Settled down to enjoy a few hours of dreams;
Half an hour off Midnight, a gate latch went 'clank',
And the first of his wagons set off for the Bank.

THE GAME

The game was afoot, and the Gold was the prize
Which would be, for the winner, of momentous size
If it weren't for the Gold being fake and not real;
But the rules of the game were quite far from ideal.

No one knew if opponents would turn up and try
To extract, pirate-like, the Gold bars passing by
In the wagons of Richards, or gather their sails
And let them unfurl when the Gold's on the rails.

If surrender of wagons en-route was demanded,
The thieves, it was thought, would be taken red-handed
While weighted with ingots of Lead dressed as Gold -
The guards lurking nearby would have the thieves cold.

This seemed very unlikely but, still, might be done
But the chances would be many millions to one
That they'd meet with success and escape out of town
While they were, with their heavy prize, so laden down.

But, if the fake Gold made its way to the train,
It was thought that it might be as well to refrain
From alerting the gang of its probable plight
By keeping the wagon guards well out of sight.

The location of where any gang member hid
Was not ever determined, and any strong bid
To find out further details was sure to alert
Everyman that he should, to new quarters, divert.

So, there was no point making an early arrest
For Police had no names and there would be, at best,
A collection of foreigners who would invoke
The excuse that it was 'little English' they spoke.

This would take a few, for some time, off the street
But, as likely as not, there'd be more left to meet
At the time of the move – they must play it by ear
And respond as they might when the action is clear.

But, at least, it was thought, that the actual time
To expect the commission of such a great crime
Would be after the Gold trains had started to move,
But the knowledge of where, it was hard to improve.

It was likely the gang had been split into sections,
With Percy the Ponce making all the selections
Of who would be acting as each section-head, and
He would keep them apart till he gave the command.

Just how many groups and the number of men
To be faced at that time would stay unknown till when
The attack would begin – counter plans must include
Flexibility, great – necessarily crude.

One advantage was held by the forces of Law -
Fore-knowledge was had of the plan and its flaw
Which required that war would keep all eyes away
From the theft of the Gold on the critical day.

But all eyes would be focussed on foiling the plot;
The Gold was protected and war would now not
Take attention away from subduing Moran
And his men and his vile and infamous plan.

For that plan had been one to set nations afire
And to raise, in their ashes, a massive empire
Of great criminal enterprise before there could be
A resurgence of Law out of catastrophe.

With the threat of such war, though it never was large,
In the mind of Moran, he'd be leading the charge
To regain and expand the great empire lost
By his wily Old Master, no matter the cost.

At some point, he would realise that he'd been foiled
And his detailed planning for conquest was spoiled;
But, for now, he'd proceed as if nothing had changed -
Moran, it emerged, was completely deranged.

Though, deranged, he might be, he was dangerous, still -
For his stock-in-trade, really, was acting to kill
Without fear or compunction – the military way -
A dangerous man but much worse when at bay.

He would, likely as not, play no part to divert
Any Gold to his coffers, elsewhere – just assert
His authority over his henchmen, then wait
Till the nation's armed forces bit hard on the bait.

Warfare would be widespread, with great loss of life,
Which would bring to the country upheaval and strife
And the time would be ripe for someone to appear
With the vision and power to set a course clear.

It was he who would have all the Gold he'd require
To buy all that he needed, all he could desire,
For running the country as he would see fit -
In his mind, he could see all the nation submit.

He would wait for a year, perhaps two, till he might,
From a well-prepared refuge, come back into sight
As the saviour of all who required his Gold -
Loyalty, he'd buy cheaply; favour dearly sold.

He would regain his place and, in military rank,
Would be elevated and display all the swank
And the swagger he thought that he ought to exhibit
And not, any thought of indulgence, inhibit.

He would gather, around him, all manner of crook
And, if ever was challenged, would do all it took
To remove anybody impeding his glory -
He'd amend, where required, any official story.

This, of course, would require that all went to plan
And that every and each hired thug, to a man,
Followed orders exactly and without delay
And that war between nations was set underway.

In his sad twisted mind, Moran thought that he might
Be beloved of all, saving them from a plight
Which he brought down himself in a plot inhumane -
His men were just greedy, Moran was insane.

He had no way to know that his plan had unravelled
As news of those documents, phoney, had travelled
To nations once anxious but now reassured
That, into a great conflict, they would not be lured.

And the Gold in the vaults of the great British banks
Was secure, and Moran's diabolical pranks
Would not threaten the Pound and all it represented
And as war between nations had just been prevented.

It was now just a case of destroying Moran
And his evil desires and, thus, thwart a plan
Which had now been reduced to a grand case of theft -
Greed and vengeance and malice were all he'd have left.

But his gang would be ruthless and ready to kill
In the action expected - there would be the will
To take riches they'd never be likely to hold
In a dozen lifetimes – they'd be deadly and bold.

Richard's wagons approached along routes designated
By plans known to few and which anticipated
Attacks in the streets though, more likely, beyond
In the countryside into which thieves could abscond.

Several tons of Lead, painted as Gold to deceive
Any forces of evil, Richards would receive
And then load on his wagons in strong sturdy crates
All behind the protection of strong iron gates.

To have moved all the Gold would have taken too long
But some visible transfers of Lead with a strong
Force of guards, some in view and a good few concealed,
Would appear genuine till their hand was revealed.

After five plodding miles to Marylebone
Across London, by wagon, on hard cobblestone,
The freight would arrive at the handsome new station
To travel northward to the hearth of the nation.

Toward Sheffield by way of the London Extension
Both of two special trains, with extreme apprehension,
Would depart as though loaded with Gold, very real,
In the hope that the fate of the fiends it would seal.

Back at Threadneedle Street, the freight wagons arrived
To be loaded forthwith with a booty contrived
To resemble the Gold which held Britain afloat
In the eyes of the world, every business and boat.

It was struggle and strain with each Lead-laden crate,
Each one loaded with ingots meant to simulate,
By the multiple millions, the great common wealth
Of the nation of Britain, delivered in stealth.

As each wagon was filled to its maximum weight,
With the guards all around it protecting its freight,
It was jerked into motion as horses were goaded
To pull on the great weight with which each was loaded.

In the still of the night, the clip-clop of the hooves
Of the horses and clank of the wheels finding grooves
On the stone cobbled streets of old London, asleep,
Rang like Big Ben with midnight's appointment to keep.

On and on, without mishap, the wagons proceeded;
The big horses straining till they had succeeded
In getting the Gold-painted Lead to the station -
Richard's stables, and rest, their desired destination.

One more transfer that night for each wagon and then,
If there'd been no attack, they would disband the men
Standing guard on the route over which they traversed -
In secret, in stages, they would be dispersed.

At the station, the railway cars forming the train
Had been loaded directly so as to sustain
The momentum of moving, with little delay,
All the counterfeit cargo, now well underway.

As the dawn was approaching, away went the last
Of the wagons, now empty, and horses well past
The onset of fatigue, likewise each of the crew
Which had transferred the Gold to its location, new.

With each railway car loaded and bolted and locked
And steam up in both engines, two special trains rocked
As they felt the strain building through couplings of steel
From the power imparted through each driving wheel.

Ever slowly, the first made its way to the end
Of the Marylebone platform from which it would wend
Its way out from the city, northward, with intent
To build up a good pace and, delay, to prevent.

The second's departures was staggered by ten
Minutes, only, and followed the first only when
It was seen to have passed by Harrow on the Hill -
It was clear once past here, but could meet danger, still.

Custody of the cargo transferred at this time -
Train guards on the lookout for hints of the crime
Which might break any moment - perhaps, not at all;
Each prepared for whatever, that night, might befall.

Several military units were out on alert,
Just in case the time came when they'd have to assert,
In a disciplined manner, by bayonet and gun,
Their authority over the thieves on the run.

Though domestic, the force that Moran had collected
Was deemed as a threat to the Realm; and, neglected
As soldiers might feel with their bored peacetime woes,
They would jump into action and vanquish their foes.

On the trains, loaded up, full of fake gilded Lead,
Some Police would be stationed and, also, ahead
At all major points outward, they'd collect to respond
And stop those who'd attack or who'd try to abscond.

Railway guards would work with the Police to advise
Them of railway procedures – always very wise
When one's rolling along on the tracks in the night
Over ground unfamiliar with oil lamps for light.

Outside the Metropolis, light must compete
With a darkness which seems to be total, complete;
There'd be so many places they might be attacked -
Any a definite clue from the felons, they lacked.

Onward, the trains trundled at moderate pace,
The first leading on while, behind, giving chase
Was the second which held, standing by the main door,
Another who'd joined them direct from the Moor.

"Kent! Is that you? A surprise, unsuspected.
It's something that even I hadn't expected."
Declared Sherlock Holmes as he spotted the man
Who took charge on the Moors to defuse a foul plan.

"He's with me, Mr Holmes, and great help he will be.
I took your advice, now the man's here with me
As a Detective Constable, now of the Yard."
Said Inspector Lestrade grinning ever so hard.

"Yes, it's me," added Kent, *"and it's much gratitude*
That I have for the words that you wrote – we'll conclude
Yet another success against evil this night
If we just keep our wits when we're facing this blight."

"I'd have liked to have Jones to watch out for our backs."
Sherlock said to Lestrade, *"He's a fellow who lacks*
Any fear of whatever might threaten the nation -
A man who would stare into death at his station."

"But Kent is no slouch when some danger comes near -
He will see it approach and control any fear.
The man isn't a hot-head who's looking for glory -
He's a credit to all in the Queen's territory."

"He has energy, foresight, ambition and drive
And will thwart any scheme that a fiend might contrive."
Kent jumped in, *"Mr Holmes, I beg you – no more*
Or you'll have me out toppling giants galore."

Lestrade laughed at this comment and stated to Kent,
"Mr Holmes always winces whenever we're sent
On official enquiries – he knows we're hamstrung
By the Law which would have unofficial hands wrung."

"We have much latitude exercising the Law
Of the land – I admit there is often a flaw
In the logic of where we must start or desist -
Overstepping the mark is what we must resist."

"We must always be able to back up a case
Brought upon an offender – the courts have to base
Any guilt upon evidence gathered, in fact,
So it helps when a felon is caught in the act."

"Well, this night may be one during which we may nab
A good many offenders – we just have to grab
Everyone by the collar and haul him away,"
Declared Sherlock, *"and put him somewhere he will stay."*

"That is true, Mr Holmes, and for you it ends there.
But the likes of poor Kent have to follow to where
Any captives are taken and question them fully."
Said Lestrade, adding on, *"And not come on the bully."*

"We must list every name and say just what we saw;
We must swear to our statements according to Law
So that others can take them in front of a judge
And a jury and, from what's been stated, not budge."

"We cannot sell our stories, embellished in print,
To The Strand or some other – we can't even hint
To the Press what we know; our hands are all tied
Till the time comes along when the felons are tried."

"We must be quite exact when we bring down a charge
Or the fellow arrested will soon be at large.
A policeman must work how the Law says he can
And must not put the noose on an innocent man."

"Quite so,!" declared Sherlock, *"But, thus, it must be.*
For you must have orders, while somebody like me
Works without such constraints but will often assist
When consulted for being a crime specialist."

"When we can be of help, Dr Watson included,
And those on the Force have been somewhat deluded,
Our contacts and odd ways can help to direct
The Police to the place they might find a suspect."

"For so much of our work is not battling crime;
It's the solving of problems by using our time
To observe what most see but do not realise
Is significant although kept deep in disguise."

"We met Kent on a case which held hints of a crime
Although we were engaged to seek out, at the time,
Some foul agent of Satan which had fear instilled -
Kent could not render help until someone was killed."

"He was hamstrung by rules and procedures and those
Who, for whatever reason, deliberately chose
To ignore his good judgement, response to delay,
But he stood up, full tall, and took charge on the day."

"We were able to help being there on the spot
And, if we hadn't been there, as likely as not,
We'd have heard of more murders before any call
To Police would produce any action at all."

"Kent knows all the ways of the Force, and its flaws,
But the man's like a hound running hard on its paws
When it's hot on the scent – he's a hunter and, so,
When he's hard on his quarry, he'll never let go."

"That, I know, Mr Holmes, but we should rest our jaws
About trials and justice and sticking to laws,"
Said Lestrade, *"and keep silent and sharpen our wits -*
Keep our minds on the job and not gossip like twits."

THE RAILS

Holmes agreed and declared there was danger ahead
For the trains had to slow and then gingerly thread
Their ways slowly for now, drivers holding their breath,
For to speed around Aylesbury Curve would mean death.

Where the trains had to slow, an attack might be staged;
It was quite fraught with danger with everyone caged
In their carriages, sturdy - Holmes said, as a tease,
"On this curve, any train might be toppled with ease."

But Lestrade countered, *"No! We have men all around
And have checked for explosives, with none to be found
And no way to get near any part of the line -
My men are all armed and, to shoot, they are fine."*

*"Both Whitehall and the Yard knew that this very spot
Was a place of potential attack; though it's not
Very likely to happen because, you'd agree,
From here, with the Gold, there is no way to flee."*

*"Any plotters would have to pick up all the Gold
From the wreck of the train and it would be a cold
Day in Hell when a thief could escape with much loot -
We would collar each man or, if need be, we'd shoot."*

*"No. The danger, most likely, is further ahead
Beyond Nottingham, maybe, where we may, instead
Of proceeding to Sheffield, go east to the coast
Onto Grimsby or Hull which have docklands to boast."*

*"They would need to be able to transfer the Gold
Onto barges, most likely, or into the hold
Of a ship which would steam off to places unknown
And this land we hold dear would be then overthrown."*

"Or so one might think, were one totally mad;
There's a nasty surprise to be had for this sad
And pathetic excuse for a man who once stood
Like a tall mighty oak, now reduced to deadwood."

"Quite so!" declared Sherlock, *"I do like the way*
You've been resting your jaws but, indeed, I must say
That your logic, unlike that which I've often found
From policemen, is perfectly reasoned and sound."

"Mycroft said men were ready to seize any boat
To prevent it from leaving such docks for, afloat
On the sea, they would still be a danger set loose -
And these treasonous felons must all face the noose."

"The Army and Navy are both in position
With plans set in place which will come to fruition
When and if any signal is given to act -
A quite nasty toll on the fiends they'll exact."

"So, the only thing that we can do now is wait
As these trains move along at a slow steady gait
With us all squashed within with the Lead from the vault
With the hope that we'll suffer a major assault."

On and on the trains rumbled past stations all manned
By Police at the ready with weapons as planned;
Signals given by prearranged lanterns displayed
Would set men into action or have fears allayed.

Tapping out, one by one, as each station was cleared,
Telegraphic staff sent coded messages geared
To have stations ahead to be on the alert
And the ones now traversed, back to normal, revert.

Up by Brackley they rumbled as northward they ranged,
Ever ready for action, with signals exchanged
Between officers aided by railway guards who
Knew the ways of the railways and showed what to do.

On through Rugby they travelled, repeating the mode
Of security signals while out, all in code,
Went electric impulses, both back and ahead,
To the ones who, appointed locations, would tread.

"*One intact.*" signalled Leicester as slowly rolled by
The first train of the pair with no danger to spy
From its pattern of lanterns arranged front and rear -
After leaving the precinct, they signalled, "*One clear.*"

Ten more minutes would pass – like an hour it felt -
Till the second train came into view as it spelt,
By its lanterns out front, that no problem exists -
"*Two intact.*" went the signal, "*All safe*" was the gist.

As "*Two clear.*" went pulsating on telegraph wire,
The passengers inside began to acquire
A great sense of frustration, especially those
Who, to meet with the enemy, willingly chose.

"*Gentlemen, keep your wits – we are more than halfway
To Sheffield with our cargo – alert we must stay
Till all stages have signalled our passage, intact.*"
Declared Holmes, more impatient than any, in fact.

"*It's a long hundred miles we'll travel tonight
And packed into this carriage without any light
To warn any attackers of what they would face
Is what we must endure, and endure with grace.*"

159

"You are right, Mr Holmes," uttered Kent, *"but it's more*
Than a fellow can stand when superiors snore
Like the rasp of a saw cutting through a great log
Interrupted, sometimes, by the croak of a frog."

"I agree," replied Sherlock, *"Lestrade is inclined*
To sound like a bull elk when asleep and confined;
But he is your Inspector, so bear with it, Lad -
We'll wake him up shortly – enough sleep, he's had."

With the clickety-clack of the wheels upon rail,
Ever northward they travelled with no thought to fail
At the task they were given, the one which they chose,
And the one to which patriots eagerly rose.

Many stations were passed – they saw Rugby go by
Manned by men, resolute, who might never know why
They were out in the cold and the dark watching trains
Passing by – they were men to whom no one explains.

They did not need a reason, they took it to be
Quite important, perhaps a great catastrophe
Which would need their attention – their officers would
Tell them what they must do and also when they should.

And if they ever asked of their Sergeant, alert
And attentive to what those above him assert,
"What are we here to do on this night dark and cold?"
He would bark right back to them, *"Whatever you're told."*

The Policeman and Soldier, the Sailor as well,
Were well drilled to take orders and always to quell
Any thoughts to know better the task right at-hand
And to always obey any given command.

Such were stationed at Leicester, the process repeated
Through stations outlying, all cold and unheated;
Then to Loughborough, further, and Nottingham north
Onto where the attackers were feared to come forth.

Still no sign of attackers was there to be seen;
It was as if the exercise simply had been
One of over-reaction. Could Whitehall be wrong?
Were the chances of theft of the Gold all that strong?

There was no way to know till the Gold trains arrived
At their platform in Sheffield, their cargoes contrived
To entice any plotters of war to appear
In the open, unguarded, their motives too clear.

Before switching to Sheffield and veering to west,
The first train had to slow as if needing to rest;
There was something amiss with the first points, at least -
Indicators said west but the movement was east.

There was no way to signal that something was wrong;
Before Sheffield was warned there'd be, coming along
On that easterly tack, the Gold train number two -
There'd be guards on the station with nothing to do.

There'd be ten minutes' grace for attackers to act
And destroy all the wires to points left intact
And remove any chance to be chased along rail -
They had only ten minutes or else they would fail.

All the points would be frozen when wires were cut;
Telegraphic connections were, too, severed but,
With the telegraph network in this nation, prime,
Messages would be slower but get through with time.

It was necessary for attackers to stop
The first train in its tracks and then, on board it, hop,
Overcome the train's crew and seal guards up inside
And then take them all east on an unscheduled ride.

They had no way of knowing their plans were awry;
They still thought that the nations of Europe would fly
Into battle and mayhem and chaos would reign
Till their leader came forth and, release the Gold, deign.

Though unsound from the outset, this dangerous plan,
All the work of one devious devilish man,
Had no way to succeed but could spread fear afar,
Destroy trust in the Pound and this Land, Insular.

By their trap set with Lead which was painted as Gold,
All the forces, official, and others would hold
A quite massive advantage when action occurred
Although details were scant - on that, all had concurred.

It was 'wait and react' for the forces of Law;
They had men on the ground and the only big flaw
Was that he in command of attackers might flee
And, to gather more forces, much later, be free.

No sign was there of him in his Curzon Street house -
There was no chance of missing the tiniest mouse
If the thing scurried anywhere under its roof -
Agents had searched through it for absolute proof.

So, the Master of Crime, was abroad taking charge
Of his force in the field which, although not so large,
Was prepared to do battle for such a rich prize -
This force would be ruthless, no matter its size.

As the first train slowed up to go 'round a sharp bend
Several toughs jumped aboard and were able to fend
Off the crew in the engine and make them all jump
Into darkness – those inside did not hear the thump.

One tough grabbed the throttle, another took charge
Of the coal in the tender and shovelled five large
Loads straight into the firebox making it roar -
He continued incessantly making them soar.

With the throttle down hard, the train picked up the pace
And it started what seemed, to those inside, a race;
They pulled at the door but they found it was jammed
For a large bolt, right into its latch, had been rammed.

They were helpless until someone opened that door
So they took up positions and knelt on the floor
Behind boxes of Lead and awaited their fate
Knowing help would be coming, hoping it wasn't late.

The second train fell to the same simple trap;
When the first one had slowed, it had narrowed the gap
To five minutes between them, the toughs in command
Thinking they then controlled all the Gold in the land.

Inside Holmes and Watson, Lestrade beside Kent,
Two more constables, armed, and a railway guard sent
To advise them of signals and company ways,
Knew the game was afoot – there'd be no more delays.

Their latch, too, was jammed but a trapdoor permitted
A way out, when needed, and Sherlock admitted
That this late precaution was truly inspired -
They'd surprise their surprisers and have them acquired.

When the trains didn't pass through the Staveley check
It was clear that the plan was to capture, not wreck,
Them and transfer the Gold – those inside knew this well
But where they'd end up, only time could now tell.

They were travelling east, as expected they would,
But this had been foreseen as a way the thieves could
Get the Gold to a port – but here they'd be ensnared -
If to Hull, things were ready; if Grimsby, prepared.

With the bait firmly taken, the watchers reported
To both of the ports but soon Hull was aborted
As being a target, leaving Grimsby the one
Likely port which would see the foul plan come undone.

Both ports were prepared with troops hidden away
Although ready to act when the game came in play.
Captain Roberts in charge at the Grimsby Docks knew
That Moran's hired men would soon come into view.

Into view they did come, by a train they acquired –
An undisciplined mob, but they had the required
Desire of having more wealth than they dreamed -
And, out from the carriage, some forty men streamed.

Outnumbered, they were, by a good three to one
But good officers know that troops can come undone
If they don't obey to orders and stick to a plan -
Defeat can well come from just one careless man.

So the troops were deployed on their bellies to wait
For the foes to bite hard on the next piece of bait
Which was coming along as two trains full of Gold,
So they thought – the troops waited, all silent, but cold.

The first train pulled in slowly, the mob gave a cheer
As one of their own, the stand-in engineer
Gave a wave and a shout to his comrades in crime,
"The second will follow in just a short time."

And follow, it did, to another great cheer.
From the ones locked within, Kent said he'd volunteer
To go first through the trapdoor, the mob to distract,
Which would give, to the Army, more time to react.

Silently to the tracks, Kent descended and saw
That his plans for distraction had one major flaw
For the mob had moved forward around the first train -
To survive, from all action he'd have to refrain.

But this did give him space to get clear of the rails
And the others, who followed, said wisdom prevails
If they now head for cover and wait until when
Captain Roberts decided to send in his men.

"We'd not wish to be taken as part of the mob."
Declared Watson, who knew that it would be the job
Of the soldiers to act without thought or regard
For whomever they met in that grim railway yard.

But the mob had found Gold a distraction sufficient
To render all plans of a very efficient
Transfer of the treasure a frivolous thought -
To the Army, this was the distraction it sought.

Captain Roberts, now certain the mob was distracted,
Had judged it was time that his plan was enacted;
He signalled his troops, some now chilled to the bone,
As he blew from his whistle, a shrill piercing tone.

At the sound of the whistle, the troops made their move
And, into Moran's men, waded in which would prove
Such a shock that they mostly gave up without fuss
Although more than a few were reported to cuss.

But a couple had managed to break free and run
And a soldier was heard to have discharged his gun
And to shout out to Watson and Kent to beware -
Watson spun 'round and then, in a flash, took the dare.

He rushed into the field which was sodden with mud
Into which several bullets would land with a thud;
His revolver in hand, though the going was hard,
He cut off the retreat of each evil blaggard.

He was one to their two but the look that he gave
Made the escapees know his intentions were grave
Even though he had slipped and was down on one knee;
He had them both cold, there was nowhere to flee.

Watson raised his revolver, his nerve holding firm
As he saw the two men drop their weapons and squirm;
And he said as he knelt on his knees in the mire,
"Stand still, both you demons, or else I will fire."

Kent ran past him and shackled them both by the wrist
And he said, *"Dr Watson's a man who'll insist*
You do just what he says or you may find wind blowing
Through bullet holes in you he's keen on bestowing."

Both men, not so tough being shackled by Kent
And beneath Watson's aim, to a docile state went
And accepted their fate, be that prison or noose -
They'd be dangerous men if they ever got loose.

Several more desperate men were attempting to flee
But the troops were deployed and they clearly could see
In the dim pre-dawn glow where they hid in the field -
Out-numbered, out-gunned, they all started to yield.

"Not much more than a whimper. Not much of a fight."
Said the Captain, his troops standing out in the light
With their bayonets urging their foes to submit,
"Our treasonous Colonel Moran must have quit."

In the melee, none noticed the steamer proceed
To the mouth of the dock, it was moving with speed
To escape to the Channel with Moran on board
But without all his men and his great gilded hoard.

In a flash, Captain Roberts yelled out to his men
To assemble the large rocket launcher and then
Send a rocket aloft to explode in the sky
To alert any gunboat that was standing by.

In one minute, the rocket was sent on its way
And it rose and exploded and made a display
Which was visible far out to sea and along
A great length of the coast – its red light was so strong.

*"Well, it's up to the Navy to capture our man.
I suppose, on the sea, they're the people who can
Bring the fellow to justice."* Captain Roberts declared,
Then to Watson he spoke of the felons he snared.

*"For a medical Doctor, you handled that well;
You were once one of us and you acted to quell
The escape of those fellows – does Mr Holmes know
What an absolute marvel the man has in tow?"*

"Not in tow, Captain Roberts, but way out ahead
Where the bravest of soldiers must warily tread."
Declared Sherlock, now running to greet his old friend,
"When this man's on a mission, he'll fight to the end."

"Now, steady on, Gentlemen, none of this mush.
What you're saying is likely to make a man gush
And go red in the face." Watson said quite embarrassed,
"I only jumped in when the men had been harassed."

"That's Watson all over." said Sherlock, impressed
At his friend's reticence, *"It is freely confessed*
That the man is a partner – we each make mistakes
But each works to correct those the other one makes."

With so many men captured, three wagons were filled;
There were several wounded but none had been killed.
They were all rather sour but one cringed in fear
From the others around him – his character clear.

It was Percy the Ponce – he had nowhere to run;
His men had signed on for a good bit of fun
And a fortune if they would just follow the plan.
They were now off to prison – they hated the man.

"Grab that one," said Lestrade, *"and beware of a knife.*
He's a demon and lives to cause panic and strife.
He has done all the bidding of Colonel Moran
And I do think he should share the fate of that man."

Handing over his prisoners, Roberts conceded
His men had an outing but, really, they needed
A much better foe that the one they had faced -
"If I was Moran I should feel quite disgraced."

With Police now arriving, Lestrade could take charge
Of the prisoners who, as their number was large,
Would be sped back to London – their comfort ignored;
Such action he normally would have deplored.

"Well, my men have endured discomfort, this night
And these traitors will have to forgo the delight
Of first-class transportation – my men will have that
While the guard's van will do for that mad Percy brat."

"Will you travel down with me?" Lestrade thought to ask
Of the pair, Holmes and Watson, who tried hard to mask
Their delight at the thought of a soft railway seat,
A boom from the sea cut off Moran's retreat.

Fired over the bow of the steamer, a shot
From a Naval gunboat put the ship on the spot
For its crew knew the next could be right amidships
And that would bring an end to its maritime trips.

The steamer was noticed to come to a halt
And its Captain, a grizzled and wary old salt,
Shouted through his loud hailer to leave him afloat
When a massive explosion ripped through the old boat.

"No one could live through that; the crew are all dead
Unless any were cats and had nine lives instead."
Said Lestrade looking seaward, *"I'd say that Moran*
Has destroyed himself after we ruined his plan."

But Sherlock made a comment while boarding the train
Back to London and sleep, *"I will say it, quite plain,*
I'd prefer to see proof of the fellow's demise -
To presume that he's dead may not be very wise."

"If the Navy can fish the man out of that mess,
I'd be happy to say, though I freely confess
I have doubts on the matter, the man is deceased
And no evil from him will again be released."

No one argued the matter for all were too tired
To go sparring with Sherlock on what had transpired;
The threat was defused and the felons detained
And from mentioning Moran, all simply refrained.

With its passengers sleeping, the special train sped
Through the countryside, everyone yearning for bed
And a sound sleep to render all weariness past
Till the train had reached London and slumber at last.

But while Holmes and Watson could go home and sleep,
Both Kent and Lestrade had appointments to keep
With a mountain of forms which must all be filled in -
And a large groups of felons all making a din.

"Get you home, Mr Homes, and take Watson along;
He's too ragged and dirty, unless I am wrong,
To send home to his wife." said Lestrade with a smile,
"I'll be busy with all of these crooks for a while."

With a Hansom then hailed, the pair would return
To the Baker Street lodgings where Watson would spurn
Any morsel of food and take off to his bed -
When he woke, it would be soon enough to be fed.

They would sleep for just hours, being excited still
At the scale of disaster avoided with skill
Which was coupled with daring to foil the plan
Of that fiend Moriarty carried out by Moran.

THE CALM

Fully rested, Holmes rose and then peered through a gap
In the curtains and, then, with a loud sudden snap,
Forced the latch on the window and opened it till,
Both his eyes and his ears, with old London, would fill.

And even the smells of the city which rose
From the streets and the gutters offending his nose
Spoke of life to this man who could value the way
That the people of London got through every day.

He just stood there, not moving, until came the noise
Of his dutiful partner, devoid of all poise
After chasing his foes through the railway yard pen -
Watson had awoke to the sound of Big Ben.

He strode over to Sherlock and stood by his side
And he gave a great yawn with his arms stretching wide
As both eyes took in all there was to behold
And the warmth in his heart overcame any cold.

"Well, my clothes are quite ruined and must be replaced
But what is that compared to what may have been faced
By so many if evil had gotten its way -
I believe, My Old Friend, we did good yesterday."

Big Ben tolled telling all that the morning was done -
It was noon, and though distant, it told everyone
The Great Heart of the Empire was vibrant with life
And would meet any danger, triumph over strife.

Watson, ever the soldier, stood straight and stood tall
With such pride in his heart having answered the call
To defend, mind and body, his nation assailed
By forces of evil over which they prevailed.

171

"That's a wonderful sound in the distance, I hear;
It's the call of this city which I hold so dear
And for which we did battle with forces outrageous -
We stood with our countrymen - comrades, courageous."

Holmes didn't respond for his mind had withdrawn
And, admitting, at times, there was need to use brawn,
He despaired of the brain which held evil within -
Was the line between goodness and evil so thin?

Having filed such a question away in his brain,
Holmes acknowledged his friend but he couldn't refrain
From expressing his thoughts in his own unique way -
Holmes never held back when he'd something to say.

"This London we live in is teeming with life
Full of passion and culture and labour and strife;
It's alive but it's mindless – a beast unrestrained -
We must keep all the evil within it constrained."

"Yes! Constrain it, we must, to let decency grow -
Anyone who'd embrace it must be made to know
That the forces of good are forever alert
And, to suffer great evil, will never revert."

Looking out upon Baker Street, Sherlock caught sight
Of a messenger running and then turning right
In toward their front door; from his satchel extract
An envelope, white, of a size quite compact.

"Watson, here's a message – I hope, not a case
For I'm just getting over our last little chase
After felons, warmongers, and Gold bars of Lead -
Perhaps we might have a few days off, instead."

A rap on the door – Mrs Hudson appeared,
Envelope in her hand – to her tenant she neared;
The message she held, which the two sleuths perused,
Said '*The threat Britain faced has, of now, been defused*'.

It was signed just with '*M*' with no address or date
But both knew that it spoke of the terrible fate
Which had just been avoided for millions who would
Never know of the danger and who never should.

"Well, that's just like my brother – the man has a gift
For the understatement of what really should lift
The emotions most people show at such a time."
Sherlock said, *"For we've beaten the Master of Crime."*

With some pride, Watson said, *"Well, that is a relief;*
What might well have developed just boggles belief.
It's a shame, in a way, that I now cannot write
Of what happened – the story would be dynamite."

"I would like to describe to the Public how we,
That is, you, by and large, had the presence to be
Quite prepared to do battle with danger so dire
That it, the surrender of life, could require."

Sherlock said to his colleague, *"We must be content*
In the knowledge that millions, to death, were not sent.
It is well we were able to do all those things -
A new century of peace is the promise it brings."

"Just think of it, Watson, the future will be
One of peace and prosperity for all, as we
In this nation of ours bend nature to our will
And the benefits won, to the whole world, will spill."

"But, perhaps, in that future," he then had a thought,
"Somebody will write of events which had brought,
 To the brink of disaster, all Europe and this
 Grand and Wonderful Menacing Metropolis."

Holmes and Watson, that evening, called in on Mycroft -
Sherlock said in a voice which was placid and soft,
"We got your note, Mycroft - we enjoyed what it bode,
 But signing it 'M' wasn't much of a code."

Mycroft looked at his brother - his lower jaw dropped -
His initial was '*M*' but resemblance there stopped;
 "The initial's correct, Brother Mine, I agree,
 But, whoever had sent you that note wasn't me!"

****

Also from Allan Mitchell

Sherlock Holmes and The Menacing Moors

The world's first Sherlock Holmes novella in expressive verse was so popular with Sherlock Holmes fans that Menacing Metropolis followed.

Also from MX Publishing

MX Publishing is the world's largest specialist Sherlock Holmes publisher, with over a hundred titles and fifty authors creating the latest in Sherlock Holmes fiction and non-fiction.

From traditional short stories and novels to travel guides and quiz books, MX Publishing cater for all Holmes fans.

The collection includes leading titles such as _Benedict Cumberbatch In Transition_ and _The Norwood Author_ which won the 2011 Howlett Award (Sherlock Holmes Book of the Year).

MX Publishing also has one of the largest communities of Holmes fans on Facebook with regular contributions from dozens of authors.

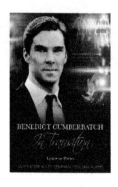

www.mxpublishing.com

Also from MX Publishing

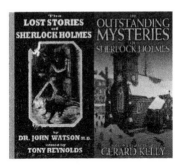

Our bestselling short story collections 'Lost Stories of Sherlock Holmes', 'The Outstanding Mysteries of Sherlock Holmes', 'Untold Adventures of Sherlock Holmes' (and the sequel 'Studies in Legacy') and 'Sherlock Holmes in Pursuit'.

London, 1920: Boston-bred Enoch Hale, working as a reporter for the Central Press Syndicate, arrives on the scene shortly after a music hall escape artist is found hanging from the ceiling in his dressing room. What at first appears to be a suicide turns out to be murder . . .

(the first in the Sherlock Holmes and Enoch Hale trilogy)

www.mxpublishing.com

Also from MX Publishing

Lego Sherlock Holmes

Seven original adventures from Sir Arthur Conan Doyle,
re-illustrated in Lego.

In this book series, the short stories comprising The Adventures of Sherlock Holmes have been amusingly illustrated using only Lego® brand minifigures and bricks. The illustrations recreate, through custom designed Lego models, the composition of the black and white drawings by Sidney Paget that accompanied the original publication of these adventures appearing in The Strand Magazine from July 1891 to June 1892.

www.mxpublishing.com

Also from MX Publishing

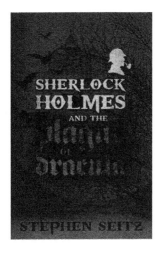

After Mina Murray asks Sherlock Holmes to locate her fiancee, Holmes and Watson travel to a land far eerier than the moors they had known when pursuing the Hound of the Baskervilles. The confrontation with Count Dracula threatens Holmes' health, his sanity, and his life. Will Holmes survive his battle with Count Dracula?

www.mxpublishing.com

Lightning Source UK Ltd.
Milton Keynes UK
UKOW06f1121051216
289223UK00001B/30/P

9 781780 928883